Drifter

RAGING HEATHENS MC, BOOK 1

CILLA RAVEN

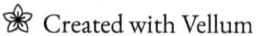 Created with Vellum

I'd like to dedicate this book to...

My great, amazing, fantastic, wonderful, awesome husband who inspires me each and every day,

North Carolina,

The trauma I call inspiration,

And to every person that had to learn how dangerous this would can be from the people who were supposed to keep you safe,

This book is for you.

Contents

Prologue

AUGUSTINE LIVINGSTON - ANCHOR

(Four Months Ago)

"They're here," Prowler said as he jumped up on the bar and slouched forward, pulling out a six-inch blade with a flick of his wrist while we waited to meet with the new leadership of The Lost Savages Motorcycle Club, who'd been our club's sworn enemy since way back in the sixties. "Let 'em in, Prospect." Prowler sounded bored as he spoke, but Emry practically bounced with excitement over the task he'd been given.

He got up in a hurry and propped the door open to our clubhouse, standing beside it with his arms crossed over his chest like a cat ready to pounce.

I pursed my lips at him.

If we had our way, no one would be fighting or dying here today unless it was done in celebration or for fun.

"Easy, Kid," our new national club president, Reaper, said in warning. Then, glancing around the room and speaking to all of us, he added, "Every one of you knows what's at stake here. Don't fuck this up just 'cause bloody knuckles give you a hard-on."

It'd been almost a decade since the last time a Savage and a Heathen met face-to-face in any official capacity, and there was no telling how long it'd been since our national club presidents gave one another the time of day.

Other meetups had occurred with the people who used to run the show, unbeknownst to the rest of our clubs, but that was one of the things we were trying to rectify today.

That underhanded, back alley shit they'd pulled wasn't okay in either of our clubs' books, and the deals they'd made behind closed doors while no one was looking went against everything we stood for. It fucked our organizations up in more than just our finances and was why we both found ourselves in such disparaging straights, having to make deals with the devils we knew just to make ends meet.

Whether we came to an agreement, an impasse, or left in body bags at the end of this, we were still making history just by reaching out for a meet and allowing them on our turf. This wasn't something to be taken lightly, and I, like the rest of our patched members, knew our club's existence was riding on this meeting. So was theirs.

A man with an inch-long graying beard and chin-length hair walked in first. From what we'd found when we'd reconned for this meeting, he was Lyn Stone, the newly appointed national president of the Lost Savages' mother chapter out of Savannah, Georgia. He was not one to cross if you wanted to keep breathing. He was just as deadly as he was cunning and unassuming.

A slew of men followed behind him, in order of their rank, while each of us stood behind Reaper in accordance with ours.

I was standing in the vice president's position while Drifter stood at my back as our sergeant-at-arms. Beside him was Cruiser, our new treasurer, and behind both of them was Brawler, our new road captain. Prowler had never done well with the ritualistic side of things, so even though he was our club's chief enforcer, he remained sitting on the bar because that was where he was most comfortable.

If anyone here could spring into action like a hairpin trigger, it was him, so we never called him out about his less-than-proper manners unless we had to.

"Reaper," Lyn said, extending his hand when he got close enough to our prez.

"Lyn," Reaper responded. "We welcome you, so long as you turn out to be what you say you are."

Lyn laughed a good-natured chuckle and spoke with an Irish/something accent I couldn't place. "Same to you, my brother, same to you." He stepped to the side so he could make the introductions. "This," he said, gesturing to the guy on his right, "is Mac. Right now, he's my VP."

He paused there, and I wondered what he'd meant by 'right now.'

Motioning to the other men in his ranks, he said, "This is Kinley, our new sergeant-at-arms; Tito, our treasurer; Ethan, our road captain; and Holden, one of our enforcers."

We all nodded at each other, and I noted each of them in turn.

Reaper introduced us, and within a few minutes, we were all sitting on different sides of the clubhouse, facing each other while the tension grew, so I had Emry bring out a round of beers for the group.

He was no more than a prospect, but he was close to earning his patch and knew better than to run his mouth about anything he heard here. So, other than his less-than-silent movements, everyone sat as still as statues for a few harrowing moments, braced for how terribly wrong this could go if we weren't careful.

"We've called this meeting because both of our organizations have had a drastic change in leadership recently. So we'd like to extend our hand to see if our long-standing feuds can be put aside once and for all, now that the old leaders are gone," Reaper said, sounding all politically correct and whatnot, which I supposed was a good thing, given the seriousness of the situation.

"Aye," Lyn nodded. "And we've agreed to see ya for the very same reasons."

"Like we discussed on the phone a few weeks back, our predecessors were up to no good, making deals behind our backs without the clubs' knowledge or vote and moving our inventory on the side to line their own pockets."

"Ours were doing the same. It's why we dinna have

much of a fight from our guys when we told 'em we were shakin' things up a wee bit." His smile was crooked and sincere, making light of the change, though I'd witnessed firsthand how out of control it could get in a club when the old, ranking members were pushed out in a mutiny like we'd had here.

At least we hadn't stripped a founding member of his patches, though. Even by our standards, that was going too far, but theirs wasn't my club, so it wasn't my problem.

"We thank ya for wantin' to bury the hatchet."

Reaper nodded before he continued. "As it stands, the Savages control the southeast, and the Heathens control east of I-95, from Maine down to the Florida Keys. We've fought the most over the southern territories since our inceptions."

"And you're wanting to maintain those boundaries?" Lyn asked.

Reaper cocked his head to the side and answered, "We're open to negotiation on that front if you are."

Leaning his elbows on the table between Reaper and himself, Lyn said, "Well, I think that depends on what you're proposin,' whether we're open to it or not."

Reaper leaned in, matching Lyn's body language as he lost his sense of propriety and spoke plainly, which was what I guessed Lyn wanted in the first place. "This is our proposal: we work together in the same territories, running different products and growing our empires simultaneously."

I didn't know if anyone else saw it, but I did - the little smirk that twitched at the corner of Lyn's bearded mouth.

"Your stronghold is in guns and black market products;

ours is in the drug trade. There really is no reason for us to be enemies. Each is lucrative and could blend seamlessly if we put aside old grudges and let them. The Savages could start running up the coast, and the Heathens could expand west."

Lyn nodded, brought a hand up to his beard for a second, then dropped it back to the table in front of him. "You make a solid point, Laddie."

I glanced at Reaper to see if the nickname upset him, but he seemed unfazed - a far cry from how our previous president would've reacted.

I sent my gaze back to Lyn with a bit of relief.

"So you wouldn't be opposed to us opening a clubhouse nearby if we make this arrangement?"

"How close is 'nearby,' exactly?" I asked.

Lyn turned his eyes to mine. "'Bout forty miles as the crow flies, VP," he smiled at me. "That island there, Topsail, the one between Wilmington and Jacksonville; that's where we're thinkin.'"

My gut reaction was to jump to anger at the fact that they'd already been casing potential properties by the sound of it, but on second thought, I knew we'd been doing the same, looking at possible chapter locations west of I-95 just in case all this went smoothly.

Reaper said, "That's really close, but I suppose, if we're working together, that could be good, so long as we all play by the rules. It would make meeting up a lot easier. Are you planning on running it yourself, moving up here?"

Shaking his head, Lyn repositioned himself in his chair.

"Nah, Savannah's my home; I don't think that'll ever change." He chuckled to himself. "My nephew, though, he's the one that'll open the probate chapter if all goes well here."

"Who's your nephew? Is he here?"

Lyn laughed again and put one of his hands in the air. "Let's cross that bridge when we get to it, aye? Nothin's been agreed on yet." He turned serious as he spoke. "The only way this'll work is if we're both lining each others' pockets, bein' mutually beneficial to one another."

"What do you have in mind?" Reaper asked as he sat back in his chair, closer to where I was.

"We can agree to the territory changes you've proposed, but we're thinking of a trade, of sorts, for our differing products. We'd like to sell you our guns and buy your drugs, seein' as how each of us has different supplies comin' in. We'll sell Heathen drugs to our established customer base, and you'll sell Savage guns to yours. If and when our territories cross, we establish Savage and Heathen-exclusive businesses, where we stay out of each other's way, and we both rake in the profits."

"Cruiser?" Reaper asked, drawing everyone's attention to our new treasurer. "Can that work?"

Chase 'Cruiser' Evans was the son of our founding treasurer, Capone, and had been one of my best friends since we were kids. He was the reason our 'crew' ended up prospecting with the Heathens in the first place roughly nine years ago.

Raised in this club from when his mom died and his father took full custody of him, he followed right in his father's footsteps when we changed leadership a few weeks back. He was far more qualified for his new position from all the shiesty shit he'd learned from his father than the guy who'd been here before him ever was because no one was more capable or faster than Cruiser at running numbers and scenarios out in his head.

The man was like a walking machine with a personality that made that kind of thing not seem out of place or weird. His permanent, charming smile spread across his face as he turned his attention from our prez to theirs. "What's the cut? 'Cause, you should know we're not getting out of bed for anything less than ten percent off the top."

Laughing, Lyn said, "Aye, we were down to go up to fifteen, Laddie, but if you insist, we'll take your ten."

"Fifteen, you say?" Cruiser said as he dramatically put a hand to his chin in consideration. "What were you gonna do with all that extra doe, I wonder." He gasped mockingly. "Oh! You need it for that ancient ass bike you rolled in on!"

As soon as Lyn and Reaper started laughing at Cruiser, the rest of the room seemed to relax tenfold, and I felt my own shoulders fall some as I breathed out the breath I'd been holding.

"You wound me, Laddie!" Lyn said as he sent his right hand to his heart. "But don't let looks deceive ya; that dinosaur could put some of those bikes I saw outside to shame."

"Don't fix what ain't broken, right?" Reaper laughed.

"Exactly."

"Well, that sums up our agenda. What about you guys?

Is there anything else you'd like to discuss before we make this treaty official?"

Standing and nodding, Lyn said, "Aye, there's just the simple matter of our tradition that's left."

"And what tradition is that?" Reaper asked, standing as well.

"There can't be a truce without a fight for good luck in our neck of the woods."

I didn't need to see Reaper's smile because I could feel it in the air, see it reflected in the eyes of all the Savages across the room, and sense it in my brothers surrounding me.

None of us were getting out of here without a fight, and as it turned out, that was exactly how we wanted it to be.

CHAPTER 1
Skye Sutton

Escape.

An escape was all I'd wanted.

From everything and everyone that used to hold me in the town where I grew up.

From myself and the memories that still haunt me, day in and day out, from that part of my life.

The memories I have?

The rage?

Yeah, those demons aren't going anywhere fast.

They've crept into my soul, made themselves at home in the cobwebs and blood in my veins, swallowed the key to my past, and laughed in my face when I've tried to help or heal them.

I didn't think I'd ever get rid of these wounds, but so be it; I am who I am because of them.

The red paint at the end of my brush slashed one of its last strokes across the brick of my new shop as my anger resurfaced, yet again, while I painted, curving around a shadowy figure with a menacing grin that looked like he ate souls for breakfast and entrails for dinner.

He was scary when I climbed down the ladder and took a step back to get a good look at him, but that was exactly what I'd been going for, and he was nowhere near as terrifying as the smiling woman he was facing in an ultimate showdown of bad versus worse.

The gleam in her eye said she wasn't afraid at all. In fact, as if she were a reflection of myself, she looked like she positively craved the violence she knew was about to take place. The decked-out Harley between her legs, shooting fire out of its pipes as she barrelled toward him with the confidence of someone who knew they'd already won.

At her back, what she was fighting for - new experiences, freedom, adventure, romance, captivation, healing... all of it... everything good this life has to offer - shined bright in the midday sun on the left side of the graffiti-style mural I was painting.

Crisp green grass surrounded an open road, flanked on either side by wasps and butterflies of every color, streaming out of the back of her bike between the flames like she paved roads of happiness wherever she went. An ever-present, fortuitous raven, following closely behind her, cawing out a warning of what was ahead, reminding her to keep her balance and to show no mercy when the worst of this world finally showed the cards in his hands.

The man was a dealer of pain, a harbinger of bad luck, poor

decisions, and evil thoughts and actions. His unyielding sights were set on her and everything she loved. Dead seagulls pecked and gnawed at his flesh, getting high on the taste of his rancid skin, seeming to endeavor to deplete him before he grabbed one and fed from it, from himself, as he stood sizing her up.

But it was a losing game for him.

The more he took from her, the stronger she became and the more light she created, making him even more desperate as time passed.

She had... I heard motorcycles off in the distance, and my ears perked up, snapping me out of considering my work. They were getting closer and slowing down, making butterflies erupt in my stomach because I might be getting my first customers.

A slow smile spread across my lips.

Today was officially my new motorcycle repair shop's first day in business, and as expected, there wasn't exactly a crowd of people waiting to get in when I opened this morning.

I hadn't advertised anything besides the big fabric 'Grand Opening on Saturday' banner I'd put out by the road on Monday. It was going to take time to build up my reputation here the way I wanted to build it, the way Trick had built the one I'd apprenticed under, but it was a task I was excited about and didn't want to rush, one I was looking forward to honing over years if need be.

The sign over the door read 'Skye's The Limit - Cycle Repair and Customization' in your typical black typography against a white background with just a hint of a flame dancing around behind the letters.

I'd originally wanted something more my style and less run-of-the-mill biker branding when I'd been putting together my plan to move out here, but when I'd run it past him, Trick had insisted I have something that appealed to the masses in the brand's identity.

However, he'd also said everything else could be what I wanted. This was why the whole back part of my shop was now a dedicated art studio with big windows, showcasing the harbor in as much detail as possible, given the old age of the building itself.

In his eyes, your first job was always to get them through the door.

"After that, just do you and let your work speak for itself." I could hear his voice in my head now, just as clear as the day he'd said it, and the thought of him alone broadened my smile even more.

In Wilmington, North Carolina, there was only one Harley Davidson dealership to handle all the bikers in and around the area, so dropping my shop at the edge of its downtown was also a strategic move my mentor had advised me to make.

I'd missed that man more than I thought I would over the past three months since I moved from Los Angeles, but he was only a phone call away if I needed him, and he knew what I was going through, why I needed to start over somewhere new.

Hell, he was the one that first suggested I make a break for it once I got the chance.

"It's not every day people like us inherit what you did, and even if it did come from your piece of shit mother, the best thing you can do is use it to make your life better. No good's gonna come from sitting on it out of spite. So rub her dead-ass face in the fact that you're doing more than she ever did, and live your life in full throttle."

He always had an answer for everything.

Even when I'd told him I couldn't leave the beach because it meant too much to me (as some sort of half-assed, last-ditch effort to get him to let me stay, even though I knew leaving was the best call), he just said there were beaches on the other side of the country too. Beaches that didn't have the looming threat of my past hanging over them like the ones in California did.

Toward the end of my time with him, he became even more insistent that I leave and start my life over, and it was pretty out of character for him, or at least, what I knew of him after living and working with him for twelve years.

At first, his insistence had hurt; it'd felt like he was trying to get rid of me and was tired of having me around, but a short time and a few arguments later, I finally realized that he was only attempting to stop me from sinking even further into the depression I'd been in and trying to get me out of that town - the place where all my wounds had been inflicted and were rotting me more and more with each day that passed.

I tried to pretend like I wasn't some overly excited little

girl with a shiny new toy when I heard at least ten bikes pulling up and backing into the motorcycle-sized parking spaces I had out front, even though that was exactly how I felt on the inside, as I nonchalantly started grabbing all my paint supplies to take them back inside.

I was undoubtedly covered in paint, but that had never bothered me. If a day passed when I wasn't covered in grease and oil or paint and paint thinner, something had gone terribly wrong, in my opinion.

As I turned the corner from the side of my building where I'd been painting, and laid eyes on the men, a small part of me sagged in disappointment. They were all in patched leather cuts, denoting themselves everywhere they went as Raging Heathens from Wilmington.

I would've been a fool to think the clubs around here wouldn't come calling at some point, but I *had* been naive enough to hope I wouldn't have to deal with them on my first day. If they were anything like the clubs I'd known out west, this wasn't merely a service call to check out the new mechanic in town; it was a shakedown of the tallest order, and I needed to be on guard, to say the least.

"Sup, Ma?" the one with the deeply tanned skin and sergeant-at-arms patch said when we locked eyes while I walked toward the wide-open garage door. "Your ol' man 'round?" His bright white, charming smile caught me off guard, but I recovered quickly once I heard the sexist shit that came out of his mouth.

The rest of his minions were closely following his lead, falling in step behind him, adding to the intimidating atmosphere they were trying to create by showing up in force like this.

It was only a scare tactic, though, nothing more. I was sure they always did this kind of thing, judging by their well-practiced movements. In their minds, they probably thought they could show up en masse to have the new mechanic feeling outnumbered, so they could then make their demands and collect the pound of flesh they felt they were owed.

They'd never met me, though.

I smirked at him with a knowing look, which caused his smile to grow impulsively wider, then I turned my face away again to set my paint supplies on the workbench on the right side of the shop.

When I turned back around, the one with the treasurer tab said, "Woah," as they made it inside and got their first glimpse of the place. I couldn't help my own smile at the look in his eyes. "This shit is sweet!"

"Thanks," I said, leaning casually with my left elbow perched on the workbench beside me.

All the men looked me over with differing levels of surprise crossing their features, sending a dose of adrenaline through my system in response, but I didn't let my demeanor waver. Believe me, you don't grow up like I did, where I did, without learning how to go toe to toe with the big bad bullies of the neighborhood when they set their sights on you.

Swinging a finger around to indicate my brand new shop with an impressed expression on his face while lowering his head to get a better look at me, the sergeant-at-arms asked, "This place is yours? You're the owner?"

Smiling as sweetly as I could, I nodded, knowing the best way to satiate a fly was with honey, not the acid I could've flung his way, even if their presumptuousness did rake against every women's empowerment movement bone in my body.

He didn't immediately start harassing me as my worst fears told me he would. Instead, he hooked his thumbs in the pockets of his fitted jeans, glanced around my shop again, and sent an appreciative gaze back to mine, passing the test I hadn't known I'd been giving him.

I walked over to him, extending my hand out for him to shake.

"I'm Skye."

There was no hesitation on his part as he sent a warm hand into mine and held my gaze. "I'm Diego. It's very nice to meet you, Skye," he said. His voice had a low, sexy, Spanish-sounding lilt and cadence, while his eyes were a rich light brown, pulling me into their depths within the span of a racing heartbeat.

This one was dangerous; for me, at least.

Our eyes lingered on each other, and our hands did the same, taking their sweet time to let go. He squeezed mine lightly, warmly, before we broke contact when the treasurer moved beside me on my right and sent his hand out in my direction.

Meeting his blue eyes immediately after leaving Diego's

light brown ones wasn't good for me either if all the tingles I felt flowing through me were anything to go by.

"I'm Chase," he said, a toothy smile spreading across his smooth face under a head of brown hair that fell in his eyes as he moved. Sending my hand to him, I could sense his happy-go-lucky manner and feel the authenticity within him as he looked at me.

"We wanted to come see what this place was all about," Diego said, drawing my eyes away from Chase and back to his. "Can't say I'm disappointed."

They were both standing entirely too close to me, but apparently, my sense of self-preservation had flown outside to hang with the raven on my wall, and in its place, an excited kind of desire had stepped up to fill the void.

"Well, I should hope not," I said with another smartass smirk as one of my hands landed on my hip. "You guys are my ideal customer, slung up in matching leather with a cherry on top, no less." I nodded my head toward Chase. "If you were disappointed, the hefty investment I made in this place would've been a crapshoot."

"Is that... Trick?" one of the guys asked, eyes wide as he walked over to the office and waiting room door, pointing to the poster-sized canvas picture I'd hung beside it.

It'd cost a pretty penny to get the image of Trick and me working together on one of the first bikes I ever touched printed, but having that time in our past hanging in a place of honor, where I could see it every day, had meant a lot to me and was worth far more than what I'd paid for it.

It was from around when Trick first found me, back

when I was just sixteen, living on the streets of LA before we both kind of went into hiding.

"Yeah," I answered.

The guy moved his gaze from the picture back to me, eyebrows high as he assessed me anew. "And that's you with him?" He didn't wait for my answer before walking toward me, and I felt everyone's focus shift my way again.

"Yep."

"That man's a legend," he said as I read the patch on his chest that identified him as their road captain. He had dark brown eyes, sepia skin, and a fresh shape-up around his short black hair, which were a beautiful, sinful combination, especially considering all the swagger he was exuding as he stalked over to me. "You're from LA?"

"Three correct guesses in a row!" I feigned delight. "Get this man a beer!"

His smile was infectious, and I could see in my periphery that the others were smiling the same way. I had not anticipated this... the level of pheromones parading around my shop, but here I was, drenched in them in their presence.

"I would love to have a beer with you," he said, accentuating the word 'love' as he spoke, causing tingles to shoot through me, just under my skin, "but this isn't a social call."

"It's a business meeting," Diego said, drawing my attention back to him.

"I figured as much." I hooked my thumbs in the back pockets of my ripped jean shorts, lifted my chin, relaxed my shoulders, and squared my stance in my thick ankle boots, opening my body language up to whatever they said.

The corner of Diego's lip twitched.

I'd pleased him with my response, but he was trying to ignore it.

"Exactly what kind of services are you offering here in our territory?"

I bit back what I'd wanted to say, probably something along the lines of, 'Can't you read?' and chose to be forthright and honest rather than snarky and impatient. "Customization, repair, detailing... the whole nine. If you need anything done on your bike, I'm your girl. I've even got a whole list up in the waiting room if you'd like to take a look. Why? You lookin' for a fix for that rusty-ass tailpipe?" I said, smirking and gesturing toward one of the bikes in the lineup outside.

I guess I couldn't help but be a little snarky.

"You can clean my pipes any day of the week, Sweetheart," Chase said, but I didn't dare move a muscle. My eyes were locked on Diego since he was obviously the one in charge, and any deviation from the bravado I was putting out there would've been seen as weakness.

Grinning evilly and stepping toward me, invading my personal space, Diego said, "You've gotta prove your chops if you wanna work on Heathen rides, earn Heathen business. Just havin' some picture of your time as a groupie from over a decade ago ain't gon' cut it."

"Groupie?" I asked, holding back a laugh. "You don't know your 'legends' very well."

"Yeah, man," the road captain said, looking at Diego like

what he'd said was an embarrassment, as it most definitely was, in my opinion. "Trick's gay, Bruh."

Diego looked over at the road captain. "Really?"

I could tell he was commenting on how the guy had busted into the middle of our conversation when he was trying to be all intimidating and whatnot, but I couldn't help myself. "Yeah, he likes dick just as much as I do," I said, unable to contain my laughter anymore. "You know, come to think of it," I added, "You're just his type. You want me to put in a good word for you?"

"I'm not gay," Diego said, unable to restrain himself from smiling. It seemed genuine, which I was immediately grateful for, and eased some of the tension I'd felt coming off of him before.

"What? You've got the guy on speed dial or somethin?'" the road captain asked with a look of disbelief on his face that matched the tone I heard in his voice.

Sobering to glance back at him, I said, "Yeah, I've worked with him for the last twelve years; we're good buddies." I knew my face had softened, talking about my mentor and the time I'd spent with him; I couldn't help it.

"Prove it," Diego said, grinning like he thought he would catch me in a lie.

Crossing my arms over my chest and leaning my weight on one hip, I said, "Sure thing. Bring me a bike to fix."

He chuckled once with no sound. "Call Trick."

"My work will speak for itself. Bring me a bike."

"Call," he said as he stepped so close the leather of his vest brushed up against my arm, "Trick."

Dropping my hands to my sides and standing up straighter, I glared up at him as I spoke slowly, punctuating every word I said. "Bring me a bike to fix."

This was the shakedown. This was where they'd chew me up and spit me out if I didn't play my cards right. I couldn't back down; I had to stand my ground. I couldn't very well call Trick up every time a customer wanted to vet me and my skills. So I'd made it my mission to make my way on my own without relying on Trick's reputation as the ingenious motorcycle wizard he is, like some snooty-ass rich kid who wouldn't think twice before climbing the corporate ladder on his father's coattails.

I was too good for that, and I damn well knew it.

"He's my friend, my mentor. I'm not gonna call him up just because some rando in leather walked in and told me to. So I'll tell you what," I said, my eyes never leaving Diego's, "You bring me a bike to fix, the one nobody else is willing to touch. You guys are bound to have at least one lying around somewhere, judging by the sorry state your rides are in. And I'll fix it. Then, after you've paid me generously for all of my hard work, then maybe, I'll call Trick and let you speak to him."

Diego and all the men in my shop went deathly still and silent. You could've heard a pin drop; it was so quiet, but I maintained eye contact, controlled my breathing, and refused to show how tingly my chest had just become. If it came down to physical violence, which would probably come at some point in this new business (such is the nature of this job sometimes), I knew I could hold my own.

Maybe not against ten pissed-off men with something to prove, but I'd go out swinging and take at least one of them down with me if I had to; of that, I was sure.

"Deal," Diego said, surprising me. "We'll be back soon."

"I close at five," I said with a smartass head tilt that had a full-on, glorious smile erupting on Diego's face.

Damn, this man was hot. I had to forcibly stop my legs from squeezing together of their own volition when he looked at me like that.

He turned around then, all of his comrades following suit. I watched them make their way across the parking lot, noting the three who chose to glance back over their shoulder at me before they rode off: Diego, Chase, and the road captain.

———

An hour or so later, I'd finished cleaning up everything I'd left outside where I'd been painting and neatly tucked it inside the shop. I closed the garage door and front entrance, then flipped the sign around that said I was out for lunch, and headed up the back stairwell to my apartment.

The old brick building I'd bought boasted a whopping six thousand square feet in total, divided in half between its two stories. My shop, waiting room, office, and storage room were a good two thousand square feet of the area downstairs, with a wall separating it from my art studio that took up the rest of the space. However, upstairs, all three thousand square

feet were dedicated exclusively to my three-bedroom apartment and even flaunted two wrought-iron balconies that hung off the back of the building, overlooking the water.

Both spaces had twelve-foot ceilings, original exposed brick walls, and old timber beams overhead. Tall windows wrapped all the way around the structure, which only irritated me when I'd been planning my mural, and I could only see the brick of my neighbor's business from inside the right half of my building.

The apartment had an open floor plan, and though I'd furnished and decorated most of the high-traffic areas and my bedroom the way I'd wanted them with the help of a designer who knew what I was going for, the rest sat empty and neglected because I didn't really know what to do with it.

I might've also run out of money.

But so what if I only had about five hundred dollars left in my bank account to last until I got some customers?

I had everything I *needed* and then some.

I even had a way to make more as time passed.

The only bills I had now were insurance, a phone payment, and whatever I used for utilities, which was far better than living paycheck to paycheck in the back of Trick's house with the mountain of credit card debt I'd been racking up in Cali.

What mattered most to me had been spending every dime my mother left me on setting my life up in ways she never did herself. By the end, I didn't want to have a single cent of hers left to my name, and by the gods, I'd done it, and done it well if I did say so myself.

Really, it was my grandfather's money that she, herself, had inherited anyway, so as Trick would've said, I needed to let that shit go.

Slapping two pieces of bread together around a slice of ham and some cheese, I stood by my oversized island to eat, staring at the four dark couches forming a giant square in my living room while my thoughts wandered to how I'd been living before I came here, how trapped I'd felt only a few short months ago.

Not only by the amount of debt I'd had, or how living in hiding had taken a considerable toll on Trick and me but also from my fear of the unknown.

Not in the traditional sense of the phrase - I wasn't scared of the dark or worried about something jumping out at me from the tree line or worrying about when or if something was going to happen. I wasn't afraid of my ability to make it on my own; I'd become a pro at that shit when I was still a teenager.

No, the unknown that scared me then, as well as now, was how to live without closure, how to move on without answers or justifications for the nightmares I've lived through, how to have this overflowing well of memories and emotions just living inside me for the foreseeable future, with no sense of justice for the ones that caused it.

I'd thought that by uprooting my life and moving to a different shore, the waves wouldn't hit as hard or pull me under so deep. However, I'd been here for three months, and

my dreams were still plagued with reconstructed, terrifying memories every night, my mind couldn't go a day without thinking about my past in one way or another, and no matter how hard I tried, I still couldn't seem to stop how my body was known to respond when I got overwhelmed by my own thoughts sometimes.

Wandering aimlessly around my apartment, sandwich in hand, I remembered the day I'd gotten the call telling me my mother had driven herself off a bridge somehow.

It was a Thursday.

I froze up on the sidewalk outside Trick's shop, lips parted without a thought in my head, as if the news had shocked me so much that even my body didn't know how to react to hearing about it.

I could see her face in my mind, hear the pinch of her voice chafing against my skin, taste bile in the back of my throat, and smell the sandalwood incense her husband used to burn as clearly as if someone were holding a burning stick of the poison, right up against my nose.

However, I hadn't been able to say anything more than 'Okay' in response to the cop that'd called me that day.

The toxicology report said she'd been drinking a lot, which was surprising considering that I'd never known the woman to have a single drop of alcohol for the entire sixteen years I'd lived with her.

She'd been real proper like that.

To the outside world, anyway, behind closed doors, she was a different human.

When I was seven, Mama married Jim - a functional

27

cocaine addict and alcoholic who could only hold down a job because he owned his own business, who beat on Mama and me every time we stepped out of line.

I used to be able to gauge when he'd fly off the handle, and it was usually whenever he bombed a job the clients then refused to pay for, or he drank too much, which was pretty much every day. It was also pretty bad whenever the house wasn't spotless, or he came up with some other frivolous excuse amid his drunken or cracked-out stupors.

However, Mama had been so wrapped around his finger that she didn't give one single fuck about how much he hurt us.

From the first time I'd complained about how he treated us, back when I was seven years old, and they were newlyweds, she'd adamantly defended him and explicitly stated what we'd done wrong to piss him off so we could avoid his wrath in the future.

Her favorite things to say were that we deserved what we got and should've known better.

Looking back on that now, I can't even begin to describe how wrong that was, how traumatizing, especially for a child, but it wasn't like I could go back and change anything; that was the mother I'd been born to, the childhood I'd been brought up in.

Well, up until the night of my sixteenth birthday, when I packed my shit, ran away, and never looked back.

The buzzer for the shop sounded overhead then, startling me out of my thoughts.

I got over it quickly and practically skipped downstairs

to the front entrance, excited again at the prospect of new customers.

Walking up, I could see Diego through the glass door, and without warning, my heart skipped a beat while a shot of adrenaline flowed through me.

I glanced at the clock on the wall above the door, noting I still had about fifteen minutes left for my lunch break, and since I knew that with these guys, you couldn't give them an inch or they'd take the whole track, I decided to play around a bit while I could, have a little fun for shits and giggles.

Pointing to the sign that was literally hanging on the door between us, I said, "Diego, I'm beginning to think you can't read." It seemed like my smile lessened the blow since he smirked back at me. "I open in fifteen minutes; you'll have to wait 'till then."

"Seriously?" he asked, shining those perfectly straight teeth at me as the sun reflected off the door between us and shimmered in his light brown eyes.

Nodding, I turned around, went to get a bag of chips I'd stashed below the cash register, pulled up one of the chairs from the waiting area so it was facing the door, and sat down, all while I thrived on the fact that Diego was watching my every move with curiosity.

Antagonizing this man was fun; I could see the twitch in his jaw and how his eyebrows had risen slightly, watching as his arms crossed and one hand went to his chin when I opened my chips and started eating them slowly, one by one.

I was playing with fire, and I knew it; I was practically

feeding off the energy he was sending through the glass and loving every second of it.

To his credit, he didn't knock or try to push me to open sooner, but he did walk to the van he drove up in, reached inside for a second, came back, and lit a cigarette. He kept his eyes on me and leaned one shoulder against the edge of the doorframe.

A few minutes later, he spoke through the door, loud enough for me to hear him. "You've got boundaries; I think I like that."

My breath caught in my throat, and I almost choked on the chip I'd been swallowing.

"And you're respecting them," I yelled back so he could hear me even though he was outside. "I know I like that."

His gaze turned hot, pointed, as he licked his lips, forcing me to cross my legs. I shoved my hand in the bag for another chip, acting like watching him wait out there was the most entertaining thing I'd seen in a while because, in reality, it was.

CHAPTER 2
Diego Melendez - Drifter

Skye's bright blue eyes were shimmering with mischief and intrigue, like the thought of getting under my skin was exciting. For a second there, it was like she was hoping I'd lash out somehow, just so she'd have a chance to react.

The little vixen.

That kind of brattiness would get her everywhere with me, and I think she'd known that from the moment we met. Still, I couldn't figure out what kind of game she was playing overall here with that much attitude and bravado.

Was it a front to seem hard and confident so the club wouldn't extort her?

That had never been our plan, but she didn't know that.

Did she think it would buy her time to get back in touch with that guy she used to know?

Trick was a legend, like Brawler said, but he'd dropped off the map ages ago, so until she proved me wrong, I was gonna think she was lying to get some kind of credit with her customers.

Was pushing limits just her thing, or did she just like fucking with me, specifically?

I had no clue.

No matter the answers to those questions, I was intrigued and determined to learn everything I could about her. I didn't even need the club's orders anymore; that look in her eye was all I needed to set that shit in stone.

When the clock finally hit its mark, she got up, slid the chair back, threw the empty bag of chips in the trash can, and opened the door for me with a gorgeous, welcoming smile.

"You came back!" she said, pulling my lips up on either side.

"You're a smartass."

"Thank you."

We both laughed.

"Did you bring me a bike to fix?"

"I did. Brought the worst of the worst, just like you said you like 'em."

"You do listen!" she said. "Two points for Diego."

"Points?" I asked as she stepped past me and pushed through the door to her garage.

"Oh, don't worry," she smirked over her shoulder, "Chase may already have five, but I'm sure you'll catch up sooner or later."

Following her and watching as she pressed a button on

the wall to open the garage door, I said, "Hold on, how does Cruiser already have five? He barely even spoke to you."

Laughing a little as my eyes rose back up to hers from her ass, she smiled hard. "He said I could clean his pipes, and he's pretty. What do you want me to do?"

Why were my palms sweating?

"Well, that's just unacceptable," I said under my breath as I went over to the back of the van and opened the doors, stepping back once they were open so she could see what I'd brought her.

Giggling some more, she asked, "And why's that?" but I didn't have a chance to answer before her eyes fell on the bike. "Aww, you brought me a Panhead!" Climbing up in the back of the van without permission, making me smile at her enthusiasm, she started touching the rusty thing all over, murmuring to herself until she finally remembered I was there. "A '53, at that! Oh, you're definitely tied with Chase, now!"

Hopping back out of the van, she grinned up at me, then turned serious.

"Alright, tell me everything you know about her and what you'd like done." Hands resting on her hips, a few long strands of her dark brown hair, which she'd left out of her messy bun, fell loose to frame her face in soft waves, drawing my attention to the stark contrast between her dark hair and light eyes.

The combination was distracting.

Clearing my throat before I spoke, I said, "Well, 'she's'

been locked up in one of our founder's garages for a while now. None of us even knew he had it..."

"*Her*," she corrected with a sly smile.

"None of us even knew he had *her* until he died, and we were going through his estate. Why is it a 'her,' exactly?"

She brushed me off with an eye roll and motioned for me to follow her as she started heading back inside her shop. "Have any of you tried to start her up?"

"Nah, we couldn't find a key."

She giggled a little to herself as she made it over to a heavy-looking metal ramp leaning against one wall and bent down to pick it up. My chivalrous side wanted me to get it for her, but another part of me said that was a battle just waiting to happen, one I probably wouldn't win, so I let her do her thing.

She was pretty strong, seeing as how she hefted the ramp, which had to be at least fifty pounds, over her shoulder and carried it like it was no more than a sack of potatoes, indicating she could probably lift a lot more than that if she had to.

"The club wants to restore it to its original glory and display it under one of our founder's pictures in our clubhouse."

"Well, that's sweet," she said, hooking one end of the ramp onto the back of the van and climbing in again. She kicked up the kickstand and slowly started easing the bike forward, aligning it with the ramp so she could get it into her shop.

The machine was rusted beyond reason, and I could tell it was taking everything she had to get it moving. Again, though, something about the determined set on her lips told me to keep my mouth shut and hands off.

My decision was rewarded as she pushed it past me - she smiled victoriously when the bike's weight finally started propelling it down the ramp without much effort.

She used its momentum to guide it over one of the inlaid, rectangular-shaped areas she had in the floor of her shop and stepped on a button beside the rectangle. We watched as a metal stand started rising from the floor and seated itself under the bike's frame, lifting it a few inches off the ground. Then the whole rectangular part of the floor surrounding the stand started rising as well, surprising me as an entire workbench popped up out of the ground.

It rose until the whole bench was at the height of her hips, then she stepped on the button again to make it stop. A metal slab then closed the hole it had all come out of, so nothing could fall down into the abyss, I guessed.

She had six of these stands, laid out in two rows of three, so she could be working on up to six bikes at any given time, and the whole place was, by far, the most high-tech and high-end shop I'd ever seen.

"Very nice," I said, drawing her attention back to me.

She smiled softly, losing some of that enthusiasm she'd had only a few moments ago.

"Yeah. I had to make it as much of a one-woman show as possible because I knew I probably wouldn't have any help for a while. There's no way I would've been able to push a bunch of dead, six hundred-plus pound bikes up a ramp by myself all the time, so I spent a bit extra on making the shop work with me rather than against me."

I nodded, knowing it had to have cost a small fortune to set this shop up, but I didn't press for more information about it, even though I wanted to. Instead, I got back to the task at hand.

I stepped up to her and said, "Consider this your audition."

She moved her body to face me, squaring her stance with all this bratty bravado that I was really starting to like about her personality.

"If you do well on this bike, you'll be honoring our founder... our whole club, and we'll reward you for it. You'll be treated well here... fairly. Fuck it up, though..." I let my voice trail off and shrugged my shoulders, hooking my thumbs in my pockets while I tried to hide the smirk that wanted to erupt on my face at the thought of punishing her.

That could be a whole lot of fun.

Taking a step closer to me, so our chests were nearly touching, she said, "Fine, but you need to know this isn't gonna be cheap, and I don't work for beers in the back of some shithook shed. Audition or not, you will pay me exactly what I deserve for the work I do."

"Fine," I agreed, unable to hide my smirk any longer; she was killing me at this point.

"Then you have a deal, Diego." She sent her hand out to

me, and I shook it, but all I wanted to do was to pull her into me, wrap her up, and carry her off to the back somewhere, so I could have my way with her.

"As do you, Skye." I could tell she was trying to hide her smile as I let go of her hand. "I'll be back in two weeks to pick it up. That should be enough time to get this one done for someone who knows Trick, right?"

I was being a smartass, and I knew it, but I was also pressing her to see if she'd crack.

Her smile turned sinister.

"Your ignorance is palpable."

Chuckling darkly, I said, "Maybe. Maybe not. We'll see."

She crossed her arms over that delicious chest and stuck one hip out, smiling as I turned around and left her standing there.

I only looked back once to see she was still watching me before I climbed in the van, coming up with as many excuses as possible to see her again as I drove back to the clubhouse.

It would be a hell of a lot sooner than two weeks from now, that was for sure.

———

"Reaper wants us at the table," Anchor said as soon as I walked through the clubhouse door. "Let's go."

Nodding, I followed my best friend and VP into the back room, where a long table with sixteen throne-like chairs were set up for club business to be discussed. It was our club's sacred space, a place that was to be honored with the utmost respect - so much so, only fully patched, voting members were allowed entry unless called upon for very rare, specific reasons or someone was cleaning or stocking it while we were out.

Already seated at the head of the table, our president, Reaper, nodded as we took our seats, acknowledging his respect for us and our well-earned positions at the table. It hadn't been a cakewalk to get here, and his head nod drew attention to the struggle we'd all gone through to get our seats. It was a tradition Reaper started doing when he officially took over six months ago, and one we all appreciated; it was a gesture we all returned as we sat down, showing respect for his contribution too.

It was one of the only ritualistic things we did as a group that Prowler could get behind - he hated all things authoritative in nature because of how he'd been brought up, and I couldn't blame him. He nodded back to the prez as he sat down next to me, that hardened look that was always on his face, not softening a bit, even as he glanced at me.

Anchor was on my left, arms crossed on the table as the remaining voting members took their seats. He sent me a look that meant we were about to discuss something serious, but that was the only indication I had to let me in on what was about to happen.

Banging a gavel that had been made to look remarkably similar to Thor's hammer, Reaper called church to order.

"Heathens," he started, "You all know there've been a lot

of changes 'round here over the last year or so, from the first hints of mutiny to now." He paused for a breath, a few of the guys nodding in his direction. "In that time, we've restructured this organization, kicked out everyone working against it, and dealt out punishments to everyone who deserved it. Of course, we also spent a lot of time and money setting up this deal with the Savages."

I perked up a little.

"Well," Reaper said with a smile, "our first official transaction is happening tonight."

Whoops, cheers, and fists pounding on the table sounded around the room as we all celebrated this victory - it had been a long time coming. Smiling, Reaper let the commotion last for a beat before he raised his hand, settling all of us down again.

"Anchor," Reaper said, sending his eyes to our VP, "I want your guys on this."

Immediately, everyone in the room knew who he was talking about: Anchor, Brawler, Cruiser, Prowler, and me. We were like a crew within the crew of this Heathens chapter and had been our own thing ever since most of us were kids. We'd grown up together, for the most part, prospected together, and when the time came six months ago, we all took some of the highest positions in the club as an unbreakable unit. We were fiercely loyal to the club itself but even more so to each other, and everyone knew it.

"Just keep that one from losing his shit." Reaper pointed a finger at Prowler, drawing chuckles out of everyone.

I sent a hand out to pat Prowler on the back a few good

times. "We'll keep our psycho in check, don't you worry, Prez."

Smiling, Reaper said, "I know you will, but I've gotta say it anyway. Nothing can go wrong on this first run; there's too much at stake."

Anchor spoke up, trying to alleviate some of Reaper's worry, which had always been Anchor's way. "We know what to do."

"I'm sure you do, brother," Reaper said. Then turning his attention back to the rest of the table, he added, "That means I need the rest of you ready for when they get to the split."

'The split' being the abandoned farm out in Burgaw where we split up our products to go to different places.

"I don't want to be there any longer than is absolutely necessary. We take what they've brought from the Savages, get the cash they got from selling our product, and divvy it all into three groups. One, headed up by you, Little Neck, will be unloading with the Risen Demons in Jacksonville as usual. Frostbite, you'll head down south to Charleston to our brothers there, and Niner, you'll go north to Norfolk to give their chapter what they need. None of those guns better sit in our territory any longer than it takes to move them, do you all understand?"

Heads nodded all around the table as we accepted our new missions.

"Lastly," Reaper said, "We need to decide on a few of the hang-arounds the next time we have church, so be thinking about how you're going to vote between now and then."

Murmurs sounded around the table from a few guys before Reaper pounded the gavel down again, ending church and dismissing everyone.

The guys and I headed up to Anchor's room to discuss the mission before we had to get ready to go, but somehow, our conversation veered more toward Skye than anything else as we waited.

"So what'd you think?" Anchor asked, sipping on a beer as he scrolled through his phone absentmindedly. "That chick know what she's doin?'"

Laughing as I pulled a beer out of his mini-fridge and cracked it open before I sat down, I said, "Honestly, I don't know what to think about her."

"So, the same as before you went to see her again?" Prowler said with annoyance. "Did you even talk to her?"

"Please tell me she's not gonna fuck up Mason's bike," Anchor said, dropping his phone into his lap so he could eye me as he sprawled out on his worn leather couch. "The prez would have our nuts for windchimes."

"Well, like I said before," Brawler spoke up, "she does have a connection with Trick, and if he taught her anything, I'm positive we don't have anything to worry about."

Cruiser was sitting in the other chair at the table across from me. "Yeah, but we don't know how well she knew him. Why didn't you press her so you could be sure she'd do a good job before you left Mason's bike with her?"

"I did press her." I smiled, thinking about Skye. "She's just got some balls on her, is all I'm sayin.' I told her this was an audition she didn't want to mess up, and she got the message, I'm sure of it."

Not everyone seemed as optimistic as I was, and I guess that was to be expected.

Wilmington didn't sport a mechanic shop at all, much less one we could depend on as a club, so we'd always had to figure out any problems with our bikes by ourselves or drive down to Myrtle Beach to get anything serious done. It was a nuisance, to say the least, so from the second we saw a new place popping up in town, the club had been keeping tabs on its progress, trying to learn everything we could about the new owner or owners.

However, we hadn't been able to figure anything out about it, even from our connections at City Hall - they'd flat-out refused to give us any information on the new business, which had initially infuriated our prez.

"That's literally what we pay them for," Reaper had complained, "to give us the information we need, when we need it. Somebody must've paid out the ass to get them to stay quiet about it."

Then he'd thought some more on the subject and came to our crew with a plan in mind, saying how this could be a good thing for the club if the person who was running the new shop also had the ability to buy out officials. Said it was our job to flush out everything we could once the place opened, and here we were.

But even after both of my interactions with Skye, I hadn't learned anything more than how she had hard and fast boundaries, liked barbeque potato chips, and seemed to know a bike's make and model when she saw one, all the way down to the year it was made.

We speculated a little more about her and her shop for a while, but in what felt like no time, we were riding as a unit up to Topsail Island to do our first deal with the Lost Savages.

CHAPTER 3
Augustine Livingston - Anchor

The ride up to Topsail was smooth and uneventful, peaceful even.

I'd always liked stopping here on our runs up to Jacksonville because the whole island seemed like it'd taken a step back from everyday life, disconnected from the hazards of the real world, and prided itself on the fact that they were on 'island time.' Which really meant no one was ever in a rush to do anything or go anywhere since a slower pace of life reigned supreme here.

Our deal with the Savages was going down at one of the small parking lots set aside for public beach access, the one at the end of Charlotte Avenue.

It was a tiny, gravel parking lot with big, prickly bushes on either side of the stairs that went over the dunes behind the bushes. There were no businesses around and only a few houses across and down the street that could get a view of what we were doing, so for the most part, it was secluded enough to get the job done.

At least, that was the plan that had been set in motion.

We were supposed to meet up with the newly appointed president of the new Topsail Island probate chapter of the Lost Savages, Declan Stone, and a few of their other members.

'Probate' basically meant the chapter was on a trial run, where they were probably being given a set amount of time to have their clubhouse up and running with enough members and prospects to make the expense of funding a new chapter worth the investment.

We weren't heading to their new clubhouse for the deal, but I was dead set on riding by it before we left the island, just so we could get an idea of how the project was progressing.

Slowing down to ride past all the people hanging out by the pier, I noticed a bunch of rowdy Marines causing a scene in and around the parking lot, but that kind of thing was typical for Topsail. They'd get lit, throw a few punches and grab a few asses, then get a taxi back to base, where they could curl up in their beds without a care in the world.

It was just their way.

Further down, we finally got to the beach access we were looking for. Five bikes were already parked on one side of the gravel lot with their riders perched on top, waiting for us to arrive, as we pulled in and started parking our bikes on the opposite side of the lot.

There was a tremendous amount of tension in the air,

but that could also be explained away easily since the relationship between our two clubs was so new, and we'd never met any of these men before. Not to mention the fact that we were going to be exchanging upwards of twenty-five thousand dollars worth of clean (no serial numbers) Glock 19 9mm handguns, thirty-five thousand dollars in cash, and two kilos of some of the purest cocaine available, straight from Columbia, so long as this deal went to plan.

Each semi-automatic weapon we were moving was worth around a thousand on the street by itself, and since there were five of us, we'd each agreed to carry five of them back to the split. We brought two kilos of coke for the exchange, with a street value of around thirty thousand a piece, which the Savages were going to pay cash to cover the difference.

As far as weapons trafficking, it was a relatively low amount of product for a high payoff and an even higher risk of jail time if we were caught. The drugs weren't much different. However, this was a test run, just as much as this new chapter was a test chapter. Our clubs were feeling each other out with this deal, seeing how the other operated, and getting an idea of how this relationship would go.

As VP, my main objective was to vet their process, product, and reliability first and secure the exchange second. The relationship we were trying to form with them was of a much higher priority than the two kilos of coke we'd brought or the money they were bringing in.

Almost in unison, we started climbing off our bikes and walking toward one another, the light from the dim, blue streetlamp casting shadows over everyone. There was a light breeze, and you could hear the waves crashing just on the other side of the dunes, but otherwise, everything was as still as could be.

It was another reason I loved this island - most of the time, it was completely dead.

A man with blonde hair and neck tattoos stood in the center of the five men and reached out a hand to me as I read his patch.

"I'm Declan, President of the Topsail Island Lost Savages."

Grabbing his hand and squeezing hard in a firm shake, I nodded. "I'm Anchor, Vice President of the Wilmington Raging Heathens. It's good to meet you."

A guy I'd seen before... I thought Mac was his name... stepped up and extended his hand. "I'm Mac, this chapter's VP."

Sending my hand to his, I asked, "I thought you were the VP at your mother chapter in Savannah?"

Smiling, Declan said, "That's a long story, but it's one we can definitely tell you over a few beers some other time."

"Why isn't your prez here?" Mac asked, a hefty dose of attitude settling on his features, which increased all the tension I was already feeling.

Not missing a beat, Cruiser, who was standing off to my right, said, "At least we didn't bring some burnt-up prospect with us." Then, angling his chin toward the prospect, he asked, "Boy, what'd you do to look like that?"

The prospect's entire right arm was covered in scars from

what looked like some of the worst kinds of burns imaginable. And though Cruiser was the one to bring it up, that kind of thing (outright dissing someone for a disability) wasn't usually a part of his character. He'd only said it because of the attitude Mac had sent me about our prez not being here.

All the Savages smiled as Declan said, "Well, he got in a fight with a fire."

"The fire won," the prospect said lightly with a shrug of his shoulders, and immediately the tension eased dramatically, as even some of my guys chuckled a little.

"Another story for another time, I guess," I said, drawing everyone's attention back to me.

"Right," Declan nodded.

"Our prez isn't here because he's setting up our distribution with the Risen Demons, ready and waiting at the drop point."

"He didn't think this meeting was more important than chumming it up with the guys you already have a relationship with?" Mac asked, and I cut my eyes over at him.

"Mac," Declan said. "I don't see this as a slight."

"I do," Mac said, eyes never leaving mine. "It's disrespectful at the very least, short-sighted at worst, and that doesn't bode well for what we're tryin' to do here."

Forcing a chuckle to lighten the mood, I said, "Believe me, if Reaper didn't trust me and my guys to handle this exchange, we wouldn't be here. And if you had any idea about how the Risen Demons run their shit, you'd understand why he had to go there instead."

Smiling again, Declan said, "I've heard stories and not good ones at that."

"Right," I clarified as much as I could. "The leader, Grizz, can love you and what you're bringin' in one day and try to off you the next just 'cause you looked at him wrong. But they're the best distributors we've got, so we have to appease 'em. I'm sure you know how these things can go."

Seeming to lose some of his ire, Mac said, "Yeah, we had somethin' like that down in Savannah for a while. Ended up havin' to find new distribution eventually."

I got the impression that Mac was only looking out for Declan and their club, so I couldn't hold that against him. Cruiser had just done the same thing.

"Alright," Declan said, "Let's see the product."

I nodded to Drifter. He turned and went back to his bike to pull out the coke we'd brought while the prospect and two other guys from the Savages went back to theirs to grab the guns and money.

Declan and I walked over to the bottom of the stairs to watch our guys work.

Cruiser counted the money in the black duffle bag. At the same time, Mac dipped a pinky into the coke and brought it up to his tongue, nodding in approval once he saw it was legit, and Drifter set about checking every pistol to make sure it was exactly what it should be.

"Are you always going to be here for these?" I asked Declan.

He nodded. "Yeah, I'll be here. What about you? Are these the guys that will always be runnin' this play?"

"Yeah," I nodded too. "Reaper wants us on this for a while."

"Then we might as well get acquainted sometime soon. How 'bout you all come back down here tomorrow? Or we can all head up your way instead since our clubhouse isn't quite ready yet."

Thinking it over, I knew it was a gesture on his part, an outstretched hand in the midst of the unknown, and I had to admit, the easiest way to get to know other bikers was to party with them.

"That sounds good," I replied. "You guys come up to the clubhouse tomorrow night, and we'll show you all some good ol' Heathen hospitality." The words had barely left my mouth by the time our guys had loaded everything up, so I sent my hand out in Declan's direction.

He shook it and patted me on the back, saying, "It's good doin' business with ya."

"Same to you."

"We'll see ya tomorrow then."

I nodded and headed back over to my bike to climb on.

All in all, it was a good deal and went off without a hitch, which I knew both of our clubs would be excited about.

Now, all that was left was getting everything where it needed to go.

CHAPTER 4
Skye Sutton

It was mid-afternoon, six days later, when I finished up with the Panhead.

Everything was clean, polished, refitted, and in perfect working order. I'd even given it a new paint job to match the old one I'd found under all that rust it'd had. So now the '53 classic looked like it should, purred like a demon kitty, and had me smiling every time I looked at it.

A few random customers had come by since Diego dropped it off, but I could tell they were just feeling me out. They only wanted their tires changed, and only one of them mentioned anything about a paint job, but he didn't want to do it 'just yet,' for whatever reason.

My best guess had been that the Heathens had this town in a stranglehold, so only the wayward, unaffiliated motorcycle enthusiast was willing to check out the new mechanic without the Heathen's approval.

Maybe that had been why I'd obsessed over the bike for

the club as much as I had. It could've also been that I was trying to prove myself to Diego and the guys... I wasn't sure. Either way, I'd hardly slept that first night, ordering replacement parts online as quickly as possible from my guy back in LA. Then, when I'd gotten it all broken down until there was nothing but the frame sitting on my stand, I'd set about cleaning everything I could like a mad woman.

In my defense, though, that was my way. It used to get on Trick's nerves, how obsessive I'd get over a new project, but eventually, he'd just come to expect it and knew I'd be out of touch for a few days while my interests ran their course.

A few times over the last week, I saw Heathen cuts ride past my shop, but since none of them actually stopped by, I had to assume they were trying to get a look-see at my progress.

The joke was on them, though, because I'd kept the garage door closed; I didn't want anyone seeing it until I was ready to unveil it.

The thought popped into my head that I should just ride the thing up to their clubhouse and blow the horn. Let them all take it in at once. Face the music, so to speak, knowing without a doubt that what I'd done would pass their test.

Before I thought about it too much, I smiled to myself as I closed up my shop (it was about that time, anyway), climbed on the newly refurbished Panhead, googled directions to their clubhouse, put on my helmet, and took off.

While I was driving the six miles to the other side of

Wilmington's downtown district, I thought about what I was wearing and how I looked, and how that might be a problem around a club full of bikers, but I was already on my way and didn't care enough to turn back and change.

I was wearing some cut-off jean shorts, a loose-fitting tank top that kept falling down my right shoulder, boots, a few bracelets, and a necklace that hung low between my breasts and belly button. My hair was going to be a mess regardless, just from wearing the helmet, but I wasn't too concerned about it since I also had grease dotting my skin in different areas that wouldn't go away any time soon.

I'd washed my hands with Goop, so they were clean, but the parts of my thighs where I'd wiped them earlier still had streaks of the black stuff, and so did my shirt, shorts, and knees.

A few minutes later, I was pulling up to a massive chain link fence that encircled a huge, three-story rectangular building with beautiful, multi-paned windows. It was obviously very old but had been renovated and sat in the historic, industrial part of Wilmington, near its deep-water port.

Immediately, I could see heads turning in my direction as I let go of the handlebars, sat back, and pulled off my helmet. However, I quickly lost all interest in them when my hair tie got caught on the freakin' thing, so my hair fell all around me when I pulled it off.

Looking down into my helmet, I started trying to get the hair tie out of the spot it'd lodged itself, right between one of the cushions and pieces of plastic, but by the time I'd dislodged it, slid the hair tie onto my wrist for safe keeping, and looked up, five men were standing by the gate looking at me and the bike I was riding with wide eyes and appreciative stares.

Diego was one of them.

"Damn, Ma," he said, pressing a code into one of those box things to get the gate to open automatically. "You work fast!"

"And do damn good work, too, by the look and sound of it," another man said. He had brown hair that was cut short and muscles for days, a smirk to rival even that of Diego's, and thick lips I could make out from here.

The gate started moving as I said, "I told you guys my work would speak for itself."

Chase laughed while the road captain crossed his arms over his chest with a smile.

Diego said, "We'll see. Pull it up out front, and we'll decide how good of a job you've done," pointing to the front of the clubhouse.

Nodding with a smirk in his direction, I did as he asked, parking it out front in one of the few empty spaces left in the long line of other motorcycles. I could tell the bikes here were situated in some kind of formation, as if they had assigned parking, but I was too ignorant of the club's intricacies to attribute any meaning to how they were placed.

When I thought about it, though, that probably meant I'd just parked in either the president's or vice president's spot, but again, I didn't care enough to dig too deep into it.

Rather, I just sat there and watched all five of these men walk over to me as the gate closed behind them. Diego,

Chase, and the road captain were the only ones I'd met before, but the other two had just as much going for them as the others.

A few people were walking about the clubhouse grounds and spilling out the front door, where there was obviously a party in full swing going on inside. A couple of people looked my way, their gazes lingering longer than I thought was necessary, but upon some unspoken cue, when the guys surrounded me, they all shifted their focus away to whatever they were doing before I'd driven up.

I cut the engine before Diego reached out a hand to help me climb off.

I ignored it with a look that said he had to be kidding me, which made that sexy ass smirk of his return to his lips.

Stepping back so they could step forward, I watched as they checked out the Panhead.

"Girl, you've outdone yourself," Chase said, putting a smile on my face, "You even got the original pipes to replace the old ones. That's what all the people we'd talked to before said would be impossible to find."

"Yeah, how exactly did you pull that off?" the one who hadn't spoken yet asked. He had 'Chief Enforcer' written on the patch across his chest and gave off all kinds of dangerous vibes with those bright blue eyes that looked like they were staring straight into my soul.

Meeting his glare with one of my own because his words had sounded like a straight-up challenge to my ears, I said, "A girl never reveals her sources. Why? Are you lookin' for more?"

"What if I am?" he took a step toward me, a few strands of his medium-length black hair falling just above his eyebrow.

This guy was intense in every sense of the word; I could feel it in my chest, but I was nothing if not entirely game for anything he threw my way. That kind of thing was my Achilles heel, my weak spot, the chink in my armor, and just by existing and talking to me like that, this man was hitting me right where I liked it.

"Believe me, Babe," I said like a smartass, "I've got all the parts you'll ever need," with a grin he blushed at seeing, which just had me swimming on the inside to know I'd caused.

The first hint of a smile lifted one corner of his mouth before he turned away from me and pretended to check out the bike again.

Ha, I laughed inside my head; I won that round.

"I'm Anchor," the one who'd spoken to me at the fence said when he walked over as the enforcer walked away. "VP of this club."

I shook his hand, trying hard to ignore the tingles that started erupting in my belly as he looked down at me. His whole persona gave off the impression that he was in control... of himself and this situation.

My cheeks got hot looking at him, but I ignored my body's reaction to him and said, "I'm Skye. It's nice to meet you."

"Why don't you come inside so we can get your payment together?" His smile was the definition of charming if I'd ever seen it; there was no way I was denying this man... these men...

What in the hell was I getting myself into? I wondered absently as I nodded and started following Anchor onto the porch.

"Prospects!" Anchor yelled over to some guys that were hanging around outside. "Get Mason's bike where it belongs, and if there's even one scratch on it when you're done, I'll personally oversee your apology to Skye here."

I felt my cheeks getting even hotter, but that reaction was nowhere near as powerful as it was when Diego stepped up behind me.

Leaning down, so his lips were just a hair's breadth away from my ear, the air from his mouth creeping across my skin like a gentle breeze, he whispered, "When we go in, stay right behind me. Don't look at anyone. You're safe with us, but I don't want to draw much more attention to you than we already have."

Pulling back so he could walk ahead, I asked, "Is it not okay for me to be here? Anchor just invited me."

His smile was devilish.

"You're allowed here because we say you are, but you haven't been claimed by any of the guys or crews yet, so it's best for everyone if we keep your presence on the low."

Claimed? Crews? What the hell did that mean?

"You get all that, VP?" I asked.

Smirking before turning on his heel to head inside, Anchor barely nodded and didn't say a word, which had me wondering if he and Diego had different thoughts on the whole who-can-know-about-Skye thing.

Still, without much choice in the matter, I fell in line behind Diego, following his every step as I tried to keep my eyes on the back of his white shirt.

Truth be told, the next five minutes that passed as we made our way through the clubhouse were pretty overwhelming.

There were people everywhere, bumping up against me. Music was blaring out of speakers I couldn't see, but even that didn't cover the whistles I heard as I passed. Still, I kept my chin level with the floor as I followed Anchor and Diego, and the rest of the guys followed after me.

Diego's back muscles were tense; I could see them tighten even more through his shirt as we moved deeper into the clubhouse. Some girls were laughing loudly, obnoxiously falling all over themselves for some dude near the bar off to our left. Then, as we were about to head into another room off the main one, somebody grabbed my ass and squeezed as if I'd had a sign on my back plastered with an open invitation for anyone who wanted to partake.

Maybe it was the stress of the situation or all the anxious excitement building up inside me. Or maybe it was just the pure audacity that pissed me off so much. Either way, as soon as my forward momentum had been pulled to a screeching halt because of some ham-handed fuck, there was no way I could control my reaction.

In that way, I'd kind of always thought of myself as a walking contradiction.

I wanted to spend all of my days covered in paint, reading a book, or working on a bike, lost in a blissful state of peace and happiness, as carefree as the wind on a stormy day. Yet I was also like a lit fuse because of all the pent-up anger and aggression I carried inside me, just waiting for someone to step on my triggers.

Not having closure for your trauma besides your own made-up attempts at therapy tended to exacerbate stuff like that.

Whipping around and glaring at the older man and his scraggly beard (which, too bad for him, reminded me all too much of my stepfather, Jim, right then), I reached out and grabbed him by his balls through his jeans, squeezing tightly as if I had every right to do so.

It only seemed fair to me.

His body went rigid, his arms lifting slightly in surrender, even as his eyes sent daggers into mine.

"Oh, I'm sorry, is there *not* a five-finger discount on other people's bodies tonight?" I asked like a smartass. "I could've sworn that was tonight!"

The club quieted some in my periphery, but I didn't care.

The guy was in no position to start talking shit, but that didn't stop him for a second. "Melendez, get this bitch before I teach her how things work around here," he said, his eyes never leaving mine.

Anger surged through me at that.

How did speaking to anyone else when I was the one who literally had him by the balls make any kind of sense?

Squeezing tighter, my eyes narrowing even further on his, I said, "Go on, teach me," as I squeezed even harder still, punctuating my words through gritted teeth as a stifled squeal seeped out of his throat for everyone to hear. I was not in the mood for this shit. "Give it your best shot."

Diego, obviously having missed the first part of what'd happened, turned around, heard what I'd said, put the puzzle pieces together, and immediately started busting out laughing; him and all the guys that had been at the fence before.

The rest of the room had fallen silent.

The dude's face got as red as a tomato, but I wouldn't relent - I had a grudge the size of Mount Everest sitting on my shoulders for anyone who took what wasn't given, and I didn't care if this rando was who I ended up dropping it on.

A few seconds into our staredown, the guy's eyes lifted from mine to find Diego's. "I will break her if you don't get her off me right now."

His tone had changed; once I heard it, it was like realization slapped me in the face.

Liquid ice crept down my spine, cooling my anger dramatically as the reality of where I was, who I was with, and what I was doing started to solidify in my mind, but being as stubborn as I was, I still didn't loosen my grip. I figured I'd already dug myself a deep enough hole; I had no choice but to see where it led.

Diego's laughter died off quickly as he came up beside me and turned serious, the men from before following right behind him, surrounding me and the guy I was manhandling.

I could feel the warmth of Diego's skin as it brushed up against mine. Luckily, all the ire I felt from him wasn't directed at me, and I made a quick note in my head in big red letters that Diego was scary looking when he'd been provoked.

"She's claimed," he almost growled at the man, and I heard an almost imperceptible gasp from all the bystanders. "Has been from the moment I met her. Keep your hands off her, or *I'll* break *you*. How 'bout that?"

Slow down, girl; I mentally screamed at my vagina when she suddenly got a heartbeat at Diego's words. I didn't even really understand what he'd said or meant.

Looking at me then, no doubt, taking in how big my eyes must have been as I stared at him, Diego said, softer than he'd spoken to the guy, "No one will touch you again while you're here, and Little Neck is sorry." His eyes slid back to the man. "Isn't that right?"

Little Neck glanced down at me with what looked like some kind of reverence that hadn't been there before, though I had no earthly idea why he would do such a thing. "I'm sorry," he said, sounding remarkably sincere.

I let him go then, trying to understand what had just happened, but Diego gently pulled me by the arm to get us back on track to wherever they were taking me. I got distracted by his touch and knew I'd have to wait until later to unpack whatever had just gone down.

They took me to another room behind the main one,

where I could see a full kitchen off to my right with a long island that stretched the length of the space. It was laden with barstools, but hardly anyone was back here. Most were out front where the pool tables and full bar were. There'd also been a stripper pole and half-circle dancefloor off to one side, but I'd been so caught up in what I'd been doing to pay it any attention.

Here, the music and mayhem weren't that loud, and I was immediately grateful for the slight reprieve from all the stimuli I was facing.

Anchor led us to a table and some chairs over in the corner, gesturing for us to take a seat. I sat with my back to the wall so I could see what was going on through the door to the main room or watch as people came and went from one area to the other. The position made me feel more in control than I knew I was in this environment.

A few seconds later, the prospects from outside rolled the Panhead into the room. Then, working together, they lifted it up into this little wooden alcove at the back of the room across from the island. Inside, I could see a picture of a man, lit by a little sconce that had been placed above it, but I was too far away to make out any details.

Once it was positioned how they wanted it, the prospects started wiping off imaginary dust, then glanced over at Anchor for what I assumed was his approval.

He nodded at them, and they scurried off with contented smiles, but as Anchor turned his attention back to us, I started to get nervous. I was here to collect a debt; I had to remember that. There really wasn't much of a reason to come inside, but here I was, sitting with a bunch of rough-and-tumble bikers who looked like they could have all head-lined a Magic Mike show if they wanted to.

"Sorry about all that out there," Diego said from my left. "The rules are different here than they are outside the club. I should've warned you more before we brought you inside."

"She held her own, though," Chase said, drawing my eyes to his appreciative smile, which caused one of my own.

"True," Diego said, but Anchor didn't seem to care too much about where our conversation was going anymore.

He focused his attention on Diego with a hostile-sounding question that had my eyes bugging out of my head. "She did a great job on the bike and seems pretty cool so far, but what in the hell made you claim her as ours before we'd even really met her?"

Ours? I wondered as my heart rate increased tenfold.

"Oh, besides making sure Little Neck didn't do anything that would have me murder him, you mean?" Diego smarted off, and Anchor's response was subtle, just a slight lift of his eyebrow and nod of his head, but I'd caught it.

Without waiting longer than a second or two, Diego answered, "It felt like the right thing to do. We can handle the consequences later. Until then, she'll be safe under our protection, and no one will mess with her. It bought us time, if nothing else. I mean, it got Little Neck to chill the fuck out in a hurry, didn't it?"

I sensed there was truth in his words and how he'd said them, but there was also some hesitation, like he wasn't being entirely forthright - some of what he'd said had been clipped as if he didn't want to say too much.

None of that made any sense to me, though. Instead, I felt a hefty dose of confusion about everything that was going on, my thoughts jumbled into a mess by the conversation, and before I could think better of it, the questions I had started tumbling from my lips.

"Murder? Claimed? Ours? Bought you time... for what? I'm sorry, but I feel like I'm intruding on something I should've never stepped foot in," I said with my hands raised. "I think I should just collect what you owe me and catch an Uber back to the shop."

They didn't respond immediately, so I started to get up, but the road captain's smooth tone relaxed me a little at his words.

"Please don't go just yet on account of us. The club and our ways are always confusing at first. However, I promise you're not in any danger here, even if what we're talking about may seem sketchy to you right now."

"'Sketchy' doesn't even begin to cover it," I said with a half-hearted grin as he subtly licked his lips - a movement that needed to be banned immediately if I were to have any hope of keeping my thoughts straight.

"It's actually kind of cute how you have no idea what's going on," Chase said, as a shocked giggle spilled from my throat. He was resting his chin on his hand, his elbow propped up on the table as he eyed me with a playful smile.

Pointing to Chase while looking at Diego, I said, "See? I told you he was the pretty one."

Diego started laughing, but the road captain seemed offended. "What? Him? No. Why not me? I'm much prettier than Cruiser, and I'm from the same town as you - that should earn me pretty boy points."

"You're from LA?"

"Yeah, moved here the summer before I started high school with these guys."

Nodding once, I relaxed and sent one of my elbows to the table. "That's cool and all, but how can I give you points if I don't even know your name, huh? Also, Diego," I turned my attention to him, "you told them about my point system? Two more points for you." I laughed while all the guys smiled at me.

I was reveling on the inside at having all their attention on me at once.

"I'm Bronx, but these guys call me Brawler," the road captain said. "And this one here," he pointed to the angry guy from outside, who wanted to know how I'd gotten the replacement pipes, "is Prowler."

"Of course, I told them about your little game," Diego said, pulling my eyes to his. "We've been competing against each other since we were kids. Now you've just gone and made it more interesting."

I felt myself blush, but I wouldn't look down. Instead, I turned to Anchor and asked, "Is there a reason you guys can't just pay me and send me on my merry way?"

Smiling some, he said, "Well, yeah. We want you to meet Reaper. He's our president and the one that'll ultimately decide if you've done a good enough job to work on Heathen bikes."

"When will he get here?"

"He shouldn't be long," Diego said. "None of us knew you were coming today, so you can't really blame the man for not being here to pass his judgment when you showed up out of nowhere."

"That makes sense, and I guess I don't mind waiting, so long as no one fucks with me again," I said.

Anchor's voice was sincere and resolute. "You don't need to worry about that at all." Then, looking around with wide eyes and a smile, he said, "Really, we should be more worried about you making it out of here without everyone fawning over you."

Confused, I asked, "And why would that happen?"

It had taken me hearing his words to piece it together, but as I looked around the room at the few people in here, I finally registered the looks I was getting. Whispers were being spoken into eager ears, smiles were being sent my way, and if I wasn't mistaken, a few of the women that passed by gave me snooty, pissed-off glares I didn't understand and certainly didn't think I deserved.

"While we're at it, would any of you care to enlighten me about this club and its rules or whatever?" I asked, trying to make sense of what was going on.

"Of course," said a hard, low, stern voice, causing my heart to jump into my throat - Prowler had been dead silent and hardly moved this entire time. He'd startled me when he spoke up, but I hung onto every word he said. "If you want to know what our little club is all about, it's pretty simple."

I nodded cautiously, but he wasn't looking at me, and he didn't continue to explain as I thought he was going to. Instead, he was staring down at a knife in his hands, his posture tense, giving me the feeling that he didn't want to look at me.

I had no idea why, but that thought hurt my feelings some.

"The club is just a big group of guys with the same interests. Our crew is one of a few smaller groups within the whole, and we rose up through the ranks together as a team. The guys at this table make up our crew, but there are others in this chapter too. We've been friends for a long time," Anchor explained as his eyes captured mine and his hand gestured to the guys around the table.

"We grew up together and joined the Heathens at the same time nine years ago when Chase, here, finally turned twenty-one. We ride together, party together. We do our best to keep each other safe when we can... protect one another from whatever comes up, if you get what I mean." His eyes widened slightly as though expecting me to question him, so he quickly added, "I mean, with the jobs we do now and then. Somebody is always there to watch our backs."

Diego let out a long sigh. I guess there was probably a lot to learn about the club, and he didn't know where to start, so he was relieved Anchor had taken the first step.

"And you call yourselves the Raging Heathens?" I asked with an arched brow, trying to keep my voice light despite feeling slightly intimidated by their presence, but even I could admit that what I'd said had come out sounding a little condescending.

Where had that tone come from?

As soon as the words left my lips, I froze, drawing back in my chair to not make myself seem weak. Still, I couldn't help but stiffen until someone answered, even as a small bubble of laughter escaped me, regardless of the situation.

"The club was named after the one thing all who join have in common," Prowler explained matter-of-factly, ignoring my amusement, his bright blue eyes focused on mine. "The word 'heathen' is someone who doesn't believe in a particular set of rules. That's us."

He shrugged like it was obvious, and I could only blink at him before asking what seemed obvious to me. "So, you're saying you don't follow the rules, but your club has rules, and you follow those?" I knew my brow was furrowed with puzzlement because the whole concept seemed contradictory, in my opinion.

Chase tried to cover a laugh across from me, and Anchor glanced at Diego briefly before meeting my gaze again. "You've been here all of five minutes, and already you see one of the issues we've had." His smile was good-natured, if not outright surprised by my assessment, as he sent his arms back to interlace his fingers behind his head. "You'll fit in well here, at least."

"I didn't know I was trying to fit in; I just thought I was gonna get paid and leave again."

Bronx spoke up. "Didn't Diego tell you that workin' on that bike was an audition?"

I nodded as a slow smirk grew on my face because I could tell where he was going with his question. "He did."

"If Reaper likes your work, you and your shop will be in with the Heathens. We'll send all our bikes to your shop whenever they need something done."

"We're not one hitter quitters, is what he's trying to say," Chase said with a knowing smile, full of innuendo. "We are establishing *relationships* now. Ones that are mutually beneficial and last for a long time. Anything less just simply isn't good enough anymore."

I couldn't help but ask, "What's the catch? What if I don't want all my clients to only be from your club? What if I wanted more than that?"

Anchor was serious again as he leaned toward me to answer. "No one said you would only work on our bikes. The catch is that there is no catch. Our club is just in dire need of someone like you, a shop like yours, that we can rely on, and we're willing to be loyal customers, so long as you're willing to do the work. We'll even send help if you say you need it."

I couldn't help but feel like I was being signed up for something with a fine print I wasn't allowed to read, but since they weren't outright demanding a cut of what I made or making any other kinds of demands, I just nodded in response.

I thought, worst-case scenario, they were going to start making demands over time, lowering how much I got paid for the work I performed, or something like that, the longer this 'relationship' with the Heathens went on, but I also figured I could cross that bridge when we got to it.

A few seconds later, none of my worries mattered since the president walked in and went straight to the Panhead I'd fixed.

CHAPTER 5
Skye Sutton

"Come with us," Bronx said, easing a warm hand on my lower back to guide me to the bike while people started flooding into the room behind the president, who had a beautiful blonde bombshell on his arm. They were smiling and talking to the group of people that had followed them in here, so they hadn't noticed us yet as we walked toward them.

Leaning down so he could whisper in my ear, Bronx said, "You know all that attitude you've got in spades?"

I just turned my head and glanced up at him with a 'what-of-it' look on my face.

"You're gonna need it with this one," he warned, gesturing toward the president with a head nod.

The president was standing on the left side of the alcove as we made it over to stand as a group on the right side.

More people were quickly filling the room, and I had to wonder what unspoken cues or text messages had gone out for everyone to be coming in here without an announcement of some kind. Within a few seconds, the whole space was filled, blocking any chance I would've had at making it to an exit if I needed to, which set me on edge even more than Bronx's warning had.

The president's eyes finally settled on the Panhead, and his body stiffened. Then he relaxed some as a solemn look spread across his face.

Was he getting teary-eyed?

The woman on his arm certainly was; she sent the back of her hand up to wipe at the corner of her eye but didn't say anything.

Clearing his throat before he moved, the president looked away from the bike like he was searching for someone in particular. But, once his eyes landed on the guys I was with, it didn't take them long to settle on me.

"You're the mechanic that did this?" he asked, his voice stern and impenetrable - I couldn't tell by his tone alone how he felt about the work I'd done.

"Yes," I said back just as sternly, fully aware of how many eyes were assessing me right then, but Bronx was still touching my lower back, so I still felt at least a smidgen of safety.

"Does it run, or is this all for show?" he asked, insulting me through and through.

I couldn't hide the look of disgust that had settled on my face for a solid breath of time as I took a step toward him in anger. Then I got my wits about me and stopped, replying while I smirked like a smartass, "That baby can go toe to toe with any bike you've got out there and give 'em a run for their money. Why don't you take it for a spin to prove it?"

"She rode it here," Anchor said, but I couldn't look behind me to see his face as he'd said it.

"Come here," the president ordered with fire lacing his tone, and I had to do what he said; there was no way around it.

I wasn't in my element here; hell, I wasn't even on my side of the country.

Had I messed up somehow by riding a dead man's bike or something?

Yes, I'd dealt with bikers before, but I'd never stepped foot inside a clubhouse until tonight, much less dealt with the leaders of those clubs, and even in those short exchanges I'd had back in Cali, it had been all business.

These people and this place didn't feel like business as usual to me whatsoever. In fact, it felt like every move I made was a test of some kind, and I wasn't sure I liked that very much. On the other hand, they obviously played by their own rules, which I wasn't privy to, so no matter how much I wanted to avoid the spotlight, I didn't have another choice.

Stepping forward the rest of the way, leaving the relative comfort of the guys I'd been with, refusing to lower my head or look down in any way, I held the president's gaze and positioned myself right beside the bike, where everyone could see me.

The president walked forward, standing squarely in front of me as he sent a strong hand out in my direction. I shook it without thinking as the flash of a camera went off from somewhere to my left.

"Thank you," he said as he let go of my hand, his voice full of respect as he regarded me. "The Raging Heathens thank you."

"Uh ah! Uh ah! Uh ah!" everyone shouted in unison, startling the fuck out of me.

I jumped back, balled my fists up, and slightly raised them in response when they all started screaming their caveman chant like that, which caused a few laughs from some people in the crowd. Still, I ignored them and returned my focus to the president once I realized I wasn't in immediate danger.

I unintentionally repositioned my body, readying myself for a fight. Apparently, my body thought it was time to run or something now, so I had to ensure my feet stayed planted where they were.

Laughing, his green eyes softening in my direction, the president said, loud enough for everyone to hear him, "You're welcome here any time, Skye Sutton." Then turning to face the crowd, he said, "Somebody get this girl a drink! Let's celebrate!"

Instantly, the whole place roared with revelry, and before I knew it, the president was guiding my hand into the crook of his elbow and leading me over to the table we'd just been sitting at while the woman who'd been in my position, fell in step behind us.

I didn't like this. Not one bit. Honestly, I wanted to

puke, but I kept telling myself it would all be over soon, so the bile didn't rise from my stomach.

We took our seats as someone turned on loud music in the kitchen area. The president sat at the head of the table and motioned for me to sit on his left. The blonde who'd followed us over here sat on his right while Anchor sat on my left. The other guys filled in the rest of the chairs, and within half a heartbeat, four beers were placed in front of me by different hands.

When I glanced up, I saw they were all prospects.

"I'm Chrissy," the blonde said above the ruckus, nodding her head at me. "And this is my husband, Reaper."

"Skye," I said in response with a forced smile.

"You don't know how much this means to us, seriously."

"I'm glad I could help, then," I said.

Drawing my attention to him, Reaper said, "I'd like to propose a deal."

Oh, here it comes, I thought - the catch.

"And what's that?"

"I'd like to make you the official Heathens' mechanic. We've never had one here that can do as good a-work as you've done before, so I want to lock you down, so to speak."

He was smiling, but all that went through my brain was what he *wasn't* saying - that no other shops existed here because the Heathens had run them out as soon as they'd done something the club didn't like.

It was a proposal and a warning at the same time. If I'd learned anything from Trick, it was that you didn't get into bed with just anybody - they had to earn your respect, just as much as you had to earn theirs - and seeing as how I hadn't even been paid yet, there was no way I was going to agree to anything.

"What would that entail, exactly?" I asked. I knew I'd gotten the gist from the guys earlier, but I wanted specifics, and Reaper was the one I knew wouldn't hold back in that regard.

Bringing his right forearm up to rest on the table in front of him, he angled his body to see me better. Or so he could be more intimidating. I wasn't sure which.

"You'll be every biker in here's go-to mechanic and even those from other chapters if they need you. You'll put out quality work like you did on Mason's bike every single time," he said with a grin like I wouldn't hear the warning laced within his words. "It also means that when we need you, you'll be there, and if we need a place to get some work done on our own, we can use your shop to get it done."

I wasn't smiling anymore. I was barely holding in my rage.

Who did this motherfucker think he was?

Standing, I reached out my hand to him, but he just looked me in the eyes, so I dropped my hand back. "It was a pleasure working on the Panhead for you guys, but me and my shop aren't going to be beholden to anyone, ever, no matter how much you smile at me or how many Heathen customers you send my way. And judging by how you already know my full name even though I never gave it to you, I'll give you a warning of my own," I said before I leaned forward a bit to accentuate my point, "Don't dig too deep into holes you don't know; you could be digging your own grave and not even know it."

I stood straight and glanced around the table, where wide eyes were all staring back at me.

"Now, if one of you could please pay me the four thousand five hundred bucks I'm owed," I pointed over my shoulder at the bike in question, "I'll be on my way and out of your hair."

"The balls on this one," Reaper laughed as he grabbed my arm tighter than I was at all comfortable with.

I glared at his hand and slowly raised my gaze back to his.

"Sit down," he said, looking up at me. "We're not done here."

Reacting on instinct, whipping my left hand up and turning my body to get enough leverage before he'd even had a chance to blink, I wrapped my hand around his throat, squeezing hard as I pushed his whole body back into his chair so his head was angled up toward the ceiling.

"Let. Go of me," I snarled lowly in his face through my teeth, not giving a fuck about the consequences of my actions.

I knew it was stupid, somewhere in the back of my mind. I knew he was this club's god or whatever and that I was literally surrounded by his devotees, but I didn't care about that either. If they killed me for this, so be it. At least I would go out standing my ground, refusing to be taken advantage of.

In the span of his next breath, a few things happened

while my fight or flight response kicked into hyperdrive, slowing everything way the fuck down so I could catalog it all, one by one.

Diego's hand landed lightly on mine, where I was grabbing Reaper's neck.

Chrissy's hands shot up to cover her mouth.

Anchor grabbed Reaper's wrist below where his hand was still tightening on my arm.

Bronx and Chase stepped into view behind Reaper's chair, their eyes laser-focused on him.

Some warm, gentle hand started guiding my face to the right.

Prowler's eyes met mine in slow motion, giving me time to notice that Anchor looked like he was ready to kill somebody. Prowler lowered his head, staring deep into my soul as his hand glided gently up into my hair from my cheek. "Hey, Little Warrior."

"We've claimed her," I heard Anchor telling Reaper, but the rest of what he said faded out and sounded muffled as Prowler's softly spoken words distracted me hard.

It was like something in my soul recognized something in his, and I couldn't help but be drawn to him like a moth to a flame. "You can let go now, Babe; it's okay."

Quickly, I looked down and realized Reaper had indeed let go of me. He was sitting there, arm in Anchor's vice-like grip, staring up at his VP like Anchor had lost his mind.

Diego's soft touch rubbed my hand gently, bringing me back to my senses as everything started returning to a normal speed. I instantly let go of their president and took a step back while Prowler guided my eyes to his.

"You're back; I can tell," he said, and I wasn't quite sure what he'd meant by that.

His hand left my cheek slowly as he turned his back on me and stepped in between Reaper and me while Chase and Bronx walked over to stand behind me.

Everyone in the room had fallen deathly quiet in all the commotion, so I could finally hear Anchor's conversation with Reaper, who'd stood up since I last looked at him.

"You know the rules, Prez," Anchor was saying. "You're the one that made 'em for Chrissy."

Reaper stared at Anchor for a second, confusion and surprise written all over his rugged features. Then, surprising me, he said, "If I'd known you'd claimed her already, I never would've touched her." Then, turning to address me specifically, he said, "I'm truly sorry."

I nodded, but that was the most I could do right then.

"Everybody get back to what you were doing," Reaper shouted, his order followed instantly by everyone in the room aside from the guys standing around our table. "Let's all sit back down and try this again."

I could tell he was still holding onto some residual anger, but then again, he wasn't acting on it in any way I could perceive, so when I was the only one left standing there a minute later, I swallowed my pride and forced myself to sit back down where I'd been before. Still, I didn't like this one bit.

"I propose a different deal," Anchor said from my left.

He was talking to Reaper and me, but his eyes never left mine. "If you agree to become our official mechanic, which I'm sure you can tell means a lot to us, we'll agree to let you set your own terms and always respect your boundaries because we're not looking to take advantage of you in any way, I promise."

"Any terms and boundaries?" Reaper asked, but I knew his heart wasn't in it anymore since he was smiling again. It was almost like he was resigned to whatever came out of Anchor's mouth, and honestly, I wasn't complaining.

"Within reason," Anchor relented.

"I can tell you right now, I will not be at this club's beck and call," I said. "I work for me and myself alone."

"We can agree to that," Reaper said.

"And like I told Diego before, I don't work for beers, and what I do doesn't come cheap at the level I do it. Whoever comes into my shop will have to pay me what I'm owed every time I do a job. It can't start to fall off later, either. So I'm not going to look the other way just because I'm your 'official' mechanic or whatever."

"That's reasonable," Anchor said, his pretty smile beginning to reform on his thick lips.

"I also don't owe this club a thing," I said, pointing a finger down on the table. "I'm not going to turn away a customer just because you guys don't like them for whatever reason."

"What if that customer is from a rival club?" Reaper asked, seeming almost exasperated at this point.

Smirking again, I said, "Then I guess that club's gonna have some pretty stellar bikes."

He chuckled hard at that and rolled his eyes dramatically. "Ugh," he groaned, "Where'd you guys find this one, huh? It's like she's the female version of all of you wrapped up in one tiny, smartass package."

That caused a round of laughs from all the guys at the table, and I found myself smiling at them, liking being compared to them for reasons I couldn't quite name just yet.

"Fine, fine, whatever," he said a moment later. "She's your girl now. I'll let you all work out the details." I didn't have a chance to analyze what he'd said before he turned his gaze back to mine. "Just be ready for tomorrow, okay? We've got a run coming up soon, and I want everybody's bikes looking and running as good as Mason's over there. I hadn't thought we'd have time before, but with how fast you got his done, I'm sure it shouldn't be a problem for you."

I had no idea what he was talking about, but I also didn't push for more information either. Instead, I just watched as he got up and started making his way back through the crowd.

However, about the time he was halfway across the room, he called out, "Pay that woman, Cruiser, and put her on retainer while you're at it! Any woman with enough balls to grab me by the throat in my own clubhouse deserves the best we have to offer."

Then, turning his attention back toward the crowd, he added, "But none of you better go gettin' any hair-brained ideas from that. I'll pop a cap in your ass so quick you'll taste it in your fucking teeth."

Everybody at the table was sharing shocked looks with one another before Diego leaned forward and asked me, "Wanna stay for dinner?"

"Here?"

"Kind of," he said with a small chuckle, "I was already plannin' on makin' dinner for me and the guys up in my room, so we wouldn't have to be around all these people tonight, but you're free to join us if you'd like."

It kind of felt like they were stalling, trying to keep me there longer for some reason, but I was definitely hungry, and since we weren't going to be eating here, where everyone was staring holes into the side of my head, I wasn't in a mood to disagree.

A few minutes later, they led me up a back staircase.

The stairs turned halfway up to go in the other direction, opening into a long hallway littered with closed doors on either side. I thought we were staying on that level for a second, but the guys turned and started walking up another staircase that looked exactly like the one we'd just climbed.

This hallway looked similar to the one below it but only sported six doors - three on either side - fewer than the second-floor hallway. The walls were dark blue, with pictures and medals hanging at various points. Intricately designed carpet covered all but the edges of the stairs and hallways, exposing about a foot of original hardwood floors on either side. Each of the hallways was lit periodically with little chandeliers, drastically opposing the biker feel of everything else in the building.

Diego went to the last door on the left and pulled out a key to unlock it, gesturing to me a moment later. "Welcome," he said with a smile, though it seemed a little forced. "Make yourself at home."

"Okay," I said as he turned on the lights.

They'd taken me to an entire apartment equipped with a kitchen, living room, bedroom, and everything.

As I walked further inside, I realized it was very fitting for Diego... at least, from what little I knew about him. Everything looked new and state-of-the-art, yet at the same time, it was uniquely his. It was as if his presence was in every detail of the space, from the smell of woodsmoke and bar soap to the medium-sized Mexican and American flags hanging side by side proudly on the wall to my left, between two family portraits.

I didn't know him that well, but by simply being in his space, surrounded by his things, I felt like I was getting to know him more intimately than any of our conversations had the ability to do so far.

Bronx, Anchor, and Chase all went right to the empty chairs around the table as I sat down next to them. At the same time, Prowler walked over to the kitchen counter and hopped onto it, legs and body turned, so all I could see of him was his profile as if he were interested in what was going on, but not by much.

While Diego started reaching into the fridge to grab

whatever he needed, it was as if some kind of bubble had burst - all the guys started talking almost at once.

"Girl!" Chase said, dramatically bringing his hands down from his hair to the table. My eyes locked onto his ocean-blue ones, and my periphery picked up the tattoos creeping down each of his arms. He was smiling genuinely, showing off an excitable personality that I really wanted to know more about. "Do you have a death wish?"

"Seriously," Bronx said, smiling ear to ear. "I mean, I like fighting more than anybody else I know, but grabbing a prez by the throat? That was just askin' for trouble."

"And don't forget how she had Little Neck's eyes buggin' outta his head, either. I'd pay good money to see that shit again," Diego said as he started chopping up some peppers on the island in his kitchen.

"You've got a quick temper, don't you?" Anchor asked, squinting his eyes as if I were a puzzle he was trying to figure out.

Huffing from his spot above the cabinets, Prowler didn't even look over at us as he said, "No, she's just got a thing against people grabbing her without permission. There's nothin' wrong with that."

"Uh," I said, dragging out the sound, taken back by how right he'd been. I could've fucking swooned. I loved it when men were that perceptive, especially of me and how I felt about things. "Ten points to Prowler."

His eyes cut over to me for a split second while a small smile played on his lips before he sent his gaze back to the island across from him, his black hair falling to his eyebrows again.

"I could've guessed that," Bronx said, pulling a giggle out of my chest.

My phone rang in my pocket, surprising me.

I pulled it out, noticing it was a California number, and got up, walking to the other side of the living room to take it while the guys kept talking in lowered voices since I was on the phone.

"Hello?"

"Ms. Landry?"

"Mr. Fitzgerald?" I asked to clarify because he wasn't calling me from his usual phone number. "I didn't think we had any more business to discuss." I was trying to keep my voice down, but I knew there was no way the guys weren't listening in on what I was saying.

"Yes, that would've been the case, but something has happened," the lawyer for my mother's estate said, hints of worry and fear in his tone.

"What?" I asked, my senses going right back on high alert for the umteenth time today.

Mr. Fitz cleared his throat. "Jim just left my office."

I felt my breath catch in my throat but pushed my worries down as hard as possible, so I could focus. "He's done that before, and there hasn't been an issue. So what was different this time?"

"He broke into my office, Skye. He and some other guys held me at gunpoint and forced me to give him the combination to my safe." I felt my left arm drop to my side as I stared out the window in front of me without really seeing anything that was there. "He took your file, Skye. He knows where you are."

"Why would you keep that kind of stuff in your office?" I practically screamed into the phone, no longer caring who heard what I was saying. Panic, sharp and unrelenting, was surging through me so thick I could hear my heartbeat in my ears. "What phone are you calling me from?"

"It's a burner," he said quickly.

"How long do I have?" I asked as I tried to think through all the terror I felt.

"I can't say. I'm so sorry, Skye. I never meant for any of this to happen. I'm so..."

A gunshot rang out through the phone, making me jump before it was picked up again, and a new voice sounded through it.

"I'll see you soon, thief," Jim said menacingly before he hung up on me.

I pulled the phone away from my ear and just kind of stared at it for a second.

I couldn't even bring myself to turn around. The lights in Diego's apartment were starting to blacken at the edges of my vision while the sounds around me began to fade in and out with them.

I knew what this was, had felt it enough times to know exactly what was happening with a painful amount of clarity, even though I was absolutely losing it on the inside - I was on the edge of one of the strongest panic attacks I'd ever felt in my life, which was only worsened by the fact that I knew the guys were staring at me, and that I was in some motorcycle clubhouse that was completely unfamiliar to me.

My breath started coming in these short little panting gasps that I couldn't rein in. My hands went to my chest in some dumb, half-assed attempt to get my breathing back under control, but of course, the motion was of no use.

"Was that a gunshot?" someone asked from behind me, sounding like they were yelling at me through a tunnel, but I couldn't even nod in response; I was just wholly immobilized with fear.

CHAPTER 6
Princeton Avery - Prowler

I was off the counter and standing in front of Skye within a fraction of a second.

Her blue eyes were distant, unseeing, and quickly filling with tears that hurt inside my chest to see for reasons I couldn't name. Combined with the way she was breathing, I knew this was a bad one - a panic attack so consuming, it rivaled even that of the ones I'd had in the past.

Recognizing the signs immediately, I sprung into action while the rest of my crew did the same with the kind of well-practiced movements one could only learn if they'd been exposed to these things as much as we had growing up.

There was a disconnect going on between her body and her mind, and that separation was causing her body to go all haywire without its regulator there to tell it to chill the fuck out.

Her mind was gone, far away from here. If I'd had to guess, I would've said she was probably seeing a painful flash-back from her past in her mind's eye. Or imagining a life-threatening scenario so terrifying that she couldn't help but see it play out in its entirety - frame by frame, excruciating detail by excruciating detail.

In my opinion, it was a shitty defense mechanism for us to evolve as a species, but one we all had the predisposition to experience, just the same.

Drifter locked the door and started turning on every light in his apartment while Anchor grabbed a soft blanket off the back of Drifter's couch and stood at the ready for my cue. Cruiser pulled up the Italian opera playlist on his phone that he swore he only had on there for occasions such as these (but we knew otherwise) and looked to me to know when to hit play. Brawler went into the kitchen, grabbed one of the bags of barbeque potato chips Drifter had been stashing as of late, and brought it over while I took on what was usually Drifter's job when I was the one losing my shit.

It was a different experience for me, not being the one freaking out, but it also gave me some much-needed insight into what she was going through.

Without touching her (because I figured that would probably only make it worse, given how quickly and harshly she'd lashed out twice tonight), I stood in front of her and repeated what I'd said downstairs only a short time ago.

"Hey, Little Warrior." My voice was soft - we wanted to ease her mind back into her body slowly, in a way that wouldn't cause any more harm than it was already doing to itself. "Hey." Her eyes still didn't focus on me, so I tried again.

"Skye."

That got a reaction; she finally blinked.

"Skye, talk to me, okay?" I said, taking a tentative step toward her, which, even though she didn't say anything, worked out exactly how I'd wanted it to because she took an involuntary step back in response. "How'd you get here?"

Another step.

"I..." she said, confusion in her tone.

"You remember. You rode up on the Panhead."

Step.

"I did, I..." she said between panting breaths.

"What color are my eyes?"

Step.

That brought her eyes to mine and the back of her legs to the edge of the couch. I could tell she was searching for the right word to answer me, but when her legs made contact with the couch, it was like she had forgotten my question completely. As if she were only able to process one kind of stimulus at a time, and even her ability to do that was shaky.

"What color are my eyes, Skye?" I asked as I took another step toward her, which had her sitting in the middle of the couch.

"Blue. They're blue," she said, and I knew the jolt from sitting down so quickly had brought her back a bit more.

Slowly sitting down next to her, I watched as her eyes stayed locked on mine, following them as I moved like they were a life raft of hope and she was lost at sea.

We stayed there for a second before I nodded my head toward Drifter.

Without skipping a beat, he came over and sat on her other side, causing her to whip her head around to see him. Her breath had started to slow by a fraction before he sat down, but his movements made it worse. He handled it quickly, though.

"Hey, Ma," he said with a quick, cocky chin lift in her direction.

While Drifter talked to her, I nodded at Anchor and sent my hands out to grab the blanket he was holding.

"Did you know Cruiser here is Italian?"

She didn't respond while I gently draped the blanket around her shoulders, but she did turn her head in Cruiser's direction when he hit play on his phone.

Instantly, upon hearing the first few notes, her whole body slumped some.

"You're back," I said, drawing her wide eyes to mine again as her breathing slowed back down to a normal rhythm. "You handled that well." I couldn't help smiling at her.

"No," she said, wincing into a sob that she tried to hide in the blanket as she brought it up to cover her face while she dropped her head into her hands. "This is not happening right now."

"It is," I said, causing another silent sob to shake her shoulders.

"But it's okay," Drifter added, sending a look of contempt at me across Skye's back. "We've all been there."

He was lying. He knew it had always been me in her position, but I didn't think it mattered at the moment.

She didn't say anything, but after a few seconds, she surprised me when she wiped her face on the blanket, stood up, walked over to stand a few feet away, and turned to face us, a fierce kind of resolve settling on her features.

"I'm sorry you all had to see that just now; I promise I'm stronger than that." She rolled her eyes at herself, but I could tell she was still fighting back her panic, tears, and sadness.

Leaning forward, so my elbows rested on my knees, I said, "Panic attacks have nothing to do with how strong you are."

She stared at me for a few beats, obviously not knowing how to respond to what I'd said.

Visibly shaking her head a little, she glanced around the room, noting all of us. "Be that as it may, I need to go. Thank you for everything you all just did; I am really grateful. I just. I have to go."

Seeming to only now remember that it was in her pocket, she pulled out her phone and started moving her thumbs around.

"Where do you need to go?" Anchor asked. "We'll take you."

Dismissing his offer immediately with a purse of her lips and a slight shake of her head, she said, "No, it's okay. I'm ordering an Uber," without even looking up.

Walking across the living room, Anchor stopped before her and quickly slid the thing out of her hands.

"Hey," she said, confusion and anger spreading across her face, "What the fuck?"

Chuckling as he smoothly put her phone in his back pocket, he said, "Sorry, Babe, but no."

"No, what?" she lashed out at him. "No, I can't have my phone, you fucking psycho? Give it back."

Crossing his arms over his chest while trying to hide that he wanted to laugh some more, he said, "You're not going anywhere so soon after all that, and definitely not until we know you're safe. It's not up for debate, either."

"Yeah, we already voted, and you lost," Cruiser said, shrugging his shoulders with a shit-eating grin as he sat back down at the table. "Sorry, Sweets."

"You have got to be kidding me." Her voice was angry, but the way her lips lifted a little at the corners gave away how much she actually liked what was going on, despite herself.

"Nope," Brawler said as he made his way over to slouch down on the couch between Drifter and me, stretching his legs out in front of him and crossing them as he brought his hands together in his lap. "We don't play around with this kinda stuff. It's in our DNA."

Skye looked put out but, at the same time, turned on, judging by the heat in her eyes as she looked around at us.

Seeming to realize she wasn't going to get her way on this, she crossed her arms under her perfect chest. "Fine," she said. "What do I have to do to get my phone and my ability to leave?"

Walking away to sit back down with Cruiser at the table,

Anchor said, "We'll still take you anywhere you need to go; you're just not going anywhere by yourself until you tell us what that phone call was all about and explain that gunshot we heard." Once seated, he finished explaining, "You can have your phone back when I'm satisfied you're not going to use it to call an Uber."

Drifter leaned forward like I was, his tone chill and nonchalant as he said, "Have a seat. Talk to us. Tell us what's goin' on, then we'll be more reasonable."

Huffing but smirking while she did it, she sat down in the armchair by the windows, crossed her grease-stained legs, and leaned to the side with a hefty dose of attitude.

"The gunshot was a gunshot. End of story." Her words were clipped, but at least she was talking. "And if you guys wanna give me a ride, I'm not gonna argue." That last bit she'd said had her smirking even more as I processed her double meaning.

She's perfect; the words floated through my head as I felt my mouth curve in her direction, and my dick jumped in my jeans.

"We're gonna need a bit more than that if you want us to let you out of this room," Brawler said.

"You better be glad you're hot, talking to me like that," she said.

Rising to her challenge and leaning forward like Diego and I were, he said, "Why? What do you want to do about it?" He'd adopted that smooth voice that got every woman wet who'd ever heard it, and seeing as Skye's legs crossed a little tighter at his words, I knew she wasn't immune to his charm.

Her cheeks grew pink while her smirk got bigger. "Wouldn't you like to know?"

"Eh, hem," Cruiser said, pulling all of our attention to him reluctantly. "I think we're getting off track here, and if I'm not mistaken, that's exactly what she wants us to do. Isn't that right, Skye?"

Smiling wide, she bounced her leg and bit her bottom lip for a second in this sexy-ass grin that gave away all of her intentions.

"Fuck," I said under my breath as I got up and walked over to hop back up on the counter in the kitchen, ensuring that I hid how hard I was as I moved.

Ignoring me completely, Anchor pried some more. "Explain the conversation you had on the phone and the gunshot."

I stared at the counter in front of me and just listened - I couldn't look at her for a while.

"I really don't see how that's any of your business," her voice had turned hard.

Anchor replied, "It's our business because you're our business now. For one, because we claimed you, so, to the club at least, you're our responsibility. And for another, you and your shop are under our protection now."

"How are either of those justifiable reasons to tell my life story to a bunch of guys I barely know? I just met you." She paused for a second. "I don't care what your club's rules are; they don't apply to me."

"Yes, they do," I said, never looking up from the counter. "You auditioned. You got the job. You even set your own terms. Like it or not, you're already in bed with this club."

She huffed. "Well, when you put it like that." I could imagine her rolling her eyes before her tone changed dramatically into this sultry lure that had my skin tingling. "I wouldn't bed the whole club because, yuck, you know? But you guys?" She paused as if she were considering each of us, but I didn't look up to watch her do it. "Yeah, I'd take each and every one of you on, for sure."

"She's doin' it again," Drifter said, and I knew without looking that he was rubbing his hands over his face. He walked past me a few seconds later to get back on making dinner, and I could guess he'd left for the same reasons I had.

It pulled a small, silent chuckle through me, knowing she'd gotten to him too.

"We can make that happen," Brawler said, his voice low, laden with confidence.

"Skye," Anchor said, "Tell us what we want to know now." He was using his big brother voice, the one we all knew better than to ignore, but Skye didn't have that kind of insight.

I glanced up to see her response with wide eyes and was glad I had when she interlaced her fingers behind her head and started bouncing her leg again, putting her chest on full display under her loose tank top.

"Why don't you come over here and make me?" One

side of her mouth twisted up deviously as she spoke, and our responses were almost instantaneous.

Anchor rose to his feet to head toward her but was blocked by Cruiser standing up and putting an arm out in front of him, blocking Anchor from moving forward. Drifter and I rushed out of the kitchen and over to Skye, meeting with Brawler once we got there. To her credit, though, Skye didn't even flinch as we stood over her and looked down at her big, green, innocent eyes, which stood in stark contrast to that grin she couldn't hide anymore.

"You're playin' with fire, Ma," Drifter said. Then he leaned down quickly, put a hand on each of her chair's armrests, and slid his face beside hers to whisper in her ear.

CHAPTER 7
Skye Sutton

"You can either tell us what we want to know, or we can get the answers out of you in a way we'll all enjoy," Diego whispered as he rubbed himself against me one good time, so there would be no confusing what he meant by his threat, causing wetness to soak into my thong at his contact with my knee.

"But here's the thing," he said as he stopped moving and his body became rigid, "I've got a feeling that talking about your past isn't going to be fun for you, and I don't want your memories of being with us to be tainted by pain unless it's a pain we inflict on you that gives you pleasure."

Without thought, lost in his words, I felt my arms dropping to land with my hands on his forearms as he talked.

"So here's what's gonna happen..." He pulled back, lifted one of his strong hands to grip my chin tightly, and looked me square in the face.

Gah, this man knew how to get what he wanted from me, I thought with a smile.

His light brown eyes and their lock on mine were sweet intoxicants as I watched him. There were specks of gold around his irises, the perfect accompaniment to the long black eyelashes sitting around them.

"You're gonna tell us everything we need to know to keep you and your shop safe. You're going to do it without complaint and without arguing. You're going to be real with us, no matter how hard that is for you, because we'll always be real with you, so it's only fair. We need to know what we're facing, so we can know how to protect you better. Do you understand?"

I nodded, unable to keep myself from smiling evilly at him.

"In return, you can ask each of us for a reward when you're done, to be cashed in whenever you want. How does that sound?" He let go of my chin and put his hand back on the armrest while I had to fight against the urge to pout about it.

"What kind of rewards are we talkin' about here?" I asked, my smartass attitude back in full force.

Smiling sinisterly at me, Diego said, "Whatever you want. Stories about our past to make us even, favors of the sexual variety... the only thing off limits is anything that involves money; we're not paying you to protect you." He laughed genuinely in my face, one of the most glorious sounds I'd heard all day.

Diego was gorgeous. Especially when he was all turned on and happy, I noted.

"Deal," I said, already plotting what I was going to ask for from each of them, which curved my smile even more just thinking about it.

He stood up, still smirking at me, then they each went back to what they were doing while I was left sitting in my own unhandled arousal. However, I had to admit I wasn't mad about it.

If they wanted to get to know me, get themselves involved in my crazy-ass life, and were going to reward me for it, too, all that meant was that I was going to have more protection when it mattered.

As selfish as it might sound, I knew I needed them on my side. I needed what they offered, no matter how much I wished I didn't.

My life probably depended on it.

So without worrying too much about how they would take what I was about to tell them, I got up and took my time getting comfortable on the couch with the blanket from earlier and the bag of chips from the coffee table.

I crossed my legs in front of me, got the blanket situated just right, opened the bag of chips, and put one in my mouth, savoring the barbeque flavor for a moment before I looked back up at all the guys in the apartment.

"It's a long story..." I said around my bite. "Everybody better get comfortable."

Diego was cooking in the kitchen, but I could tell he was listening intently to everything that was going on. Anchor and Chase brought their chairs over and sat them in front of the entertainment center so they could be closer to hear what I had to say while Bronx and Prowler sat on the couch with me. Prowler was leaning forward to rest his elbows on his knees so he could see past Bronx, even though he wasn't looking at me right now.

Instead, his focus was on the carpet, I thought.

"I hate that I have to do this, but the only way for you all to understand what I'm facing, or who fired that gun on the phone, is to basically hear my life story."

"We've got all the time in the world for you, Sweets. Don't worry," Chase said, drawing a small smile to my lips.

Nodding, I took a deep breath and started. "My real dad has never been in the picture." Immediately, nerves started tingling in my stomach, but I ignored them. "The most my mom ever told me about him was that he was a biker guy she'd had a one-night-stand with and that she couldn't get in touch with him, even if she wanted to."

"That sucks," Diego said from the kitchen as he put a lid on a pot that was warming up on the stove.

I nodded again and kept going.

"So it was just my mom and me for the first seven years of my life." A small sigh seeped out of me as I recalled some of the good memories I had from that time but quickly dismissed them so I wouldn't start crying again.

"Then she married Jim."

A lump started forming in my throat from talking about him out loud to people that weren't Trick.

"He's a piece of shit person and an even worse stepdad.

He did things..." my voice trailed off for a second before I squared my shoulders, closed my eyes, and spit it out. "He used to take all of his frustrations out on Mama and me, so I got pretty used to knowing how to take a punch."

I didn't look up, but I went on since no one said anything.

"He owned a company that drove trucks around and filled up vending machines." I rolled my eyes. "It was one of those get-rich-quick things he'd heard about and bought into before he married my mom, and because he made his own rules, he broke them whenever he wanted to. Sometimes he'd forget about a machine and get pissed off whenever the company called him about restocking it, and a lot of times, they'd flat-out refuse to pay him and tell him to come to get his machine because they were fed up with his bullshit. He'd get piss drunk or snort his weight in cocaine over the next month or so, and that was when he'd act up the most with Mama and me."

Waving a dismissive hand, I rolled my eyes at myself again.

"Anyway, I'm getting off track." I tried to clear my throat, but it didn't work. "My mom was under his thumb in every way. She'd defend him when he hit us, call me stupid for doing things I knew would piss him off, the whole nine. He took every paycheck she ever earned from the art museum, and didn't allow her to have her own bank account, much less make any decisions on her own without his 'approval.'"

I used half-assed air quotes with one of my hands.

"One time, I remember asking her if we could go out to dinner for a change since Jim was out with his drinking buddies. She'd said she had to ask Jim and tried to call him, but of course, he didn't answer, so instead of going out with me or even deciding to eat at home, she just sat there for hours, waiting for him to call her back. I ended up putting a slice of cheese on a piece of bread and microwaving it so I had something to eat. When I went to bed that night, she was still just waiting there in the living room with her phone in her hand."

I wanted to puke, but then again, I could smell something delicious coming from the kitchen as Diego pulled up a chair beside Chase while I assumed he waited for whatever he was cooking to get done.

"Anyway, that was my life until I turned sixteen."

I paused, trying to get the courage to explain everything else they needed to know.

"How old are you now?" Anchor asked, providing me a much-needed, momentary distraction from my own thoughts.

"Twenty-eight."

He nodded.

"The day I turned sixteen was supposed to be this big thing because I was finally allowed to have friends over for a party because Jim was going to be camping. I went to school as soon as my mother told me it was okay and immediately enlisted the help of my best friend, Judy. She helped me organize everything, from handing out invitations we'd made during class, bringing over her blacklights, and even using her mom's money to order enough pizza to feed a mob. We cleared a space for a makeshift dance floor, and in my head, I knew we'd thought of everything.

The house had been packed that night. All of us teenagers squeezing into every corner of my old, tiny, two-bedroom house. Music was blaring, people were playing a game of Twister that someone had brought, and I'd just started dancing with the quarterback.

Up to that point, it had been the best night of my life, but then somebody cut the stereo off, and the lights were back on all of a sudden, blinding me before I heard Jim yelling out over all the confusion." Mocking him in my best Jim voice, I repeated what he'd said that night. "Everybody out! Who said you could come in my house?"

Then turning my voice back to my own, I said, "That kind of thing."

A few of the guys nodded in my periphery, but I couldn't look at them while I was talking - it made me feel too exposed.

"Everyone left, and Mama came inside from that sewing building she had out back that she'd always lock herself inside whenever she didn't want to endure being a mother."

Yep, I was definitely still bitter.

"But when she got in there, all she did was look at Jim like a lost puppy who'd just found its owner, trying to talk him down all over again, but it didn't work. It never did."

I paused, knowing I was getting to the worst part and didn't really know how to say it out loud. Better to just say it fast and get it over with, like ripping off a bandage, I thought before I took another deep breath.

"I'd been watching Judy drive off in her mom's pickup, but right after I closed the door, I turned around just in time to be blindsided by this haymaker he sent at my ear that knocked me to the floor. He'd never hit me anywhere that could've been seen outside my clothes before, and I didn't have time to overthink it because that's when he mounted me. He started hitting me over and over again while I tried to block his blows, and Mama yelled something about it being my birthday. I couldn't think of anything else to do, so I yelled in his face that I would go to the cops and tell them about that guy he'd killed on his truck route if he didn't stop right then."

I stopped for a second, realizing they had no idea what I was talking about, then I tried to clarify. "I don't remember why he'd taken me with him that day, but one time, when I was like ten or so, he took me with him and made me stay in the passenger seat while he did what he had to do. The next thing I knew, the guy he'd gone inside to talk to, ran out, looking over his shoulder, and then Jim stepped out behind him, pointed a gun at the guy's back, and pulled the trigger. The guy fell beside me on the pavement where I was sitting in the truck."

I sighed again.

"I'd kept his secret the rest of the time I lived with them, never mentioning it because I was terrified of him. Scared he'd do the same to me. But that night..." I paused, "Like I said, I didn't know what else to do to get him off me."

"Makes sense," Chase said, his tone soft, understanding.

"But after I threatened him, that only set him off more. He grabbed my wrists, and all I could smell was alcohol." My whole body shivered beneath the blanket, so I pulled it tighter. "Let's just say he took what he wanted after that."

"Wasn't your mom there?" Bronx asked, looking positively murderous himself.

I stared at him for a second as the memory of her, horrified, turning around and running out the back door, went through my head, and a tear broke free to run down my cheek when I blinked.

"She ran out when she saw what he was about to do." My voice came out with no emotion because to give any away with those words, in this moment, would've had the damn I was holding it all back with bursting at the seams.

The guys were looking at me now, so I sent my gaze back to the forgotten chip bag in my hands.

"When he was done, he threatened me. He said he'd finish me off once he was done handling my mother. Then he went outside to Mama's sewing building." I took another breath. "I got up, grabbed a book bag, packed my shit, and ran away that night."

No one said anything, so I kept going.

"I wanted to stay with Judy, but her mom wouldn't let me, so I ended up just living on the streets for a while. I stopped going to school because all I could focus on was surviving, and there at one point, I'd been so close to starving I really thought that was gonna be it for me.

I'd been hanging around this biker shop, hoping I'd

recognize my father... or somebody who looked like me, I guess, but I never saw anyone like that. Of course, now I know it was just a kid's naive hopefulness and blind optimism that made me stay around that area, but whatever.

That time of my life... It was hard, and I did things I swore I'd never do again, just so I had food to eat and a place to sleep where I wouldn't get snatched or worse."

I repositioned myself on the couch.

"That was where I met Trick.

He kept seeing me hanging around his shop, and at first, he told me to get lost, just like he did with all the other street kids. After a while, though, when I wouldn't stop showing up, he started giving me his leftovers 'cause he said I was 'skinny as fuck,' then he sent me on an errand here and there to get me out of his hair, and the next thing I knew, I was his apprentice, and loving every second of it.

He homeschooled me once he let me move into his spare bedroom and taught me everything he could about being a motorcycle mechanic. He made sure I got both my license and my motorcycle license... everything I needed; he stayed after me and ensured I got it on my own. He said I wouldn't learn anything if someone did it all for me."

I laughed a little at my memories of that time, and when I looked up, Bronx smiled back at me. We shared a moment there because at least he had an idea of who I was talking about, but then I tried to finish up what I was telling them because I was tired of talking.

"Trick really hated being the best mechanic in the country, though. Hated the spotlight and attention. So one day, we were working on this Ninja with the garage doors up, and Jim walked by. As soon as he saw me, he went after me, yelling about this, that, and the other, but then Trick's security got rid of him, and Trick said we needed to move, for both our sakes.

Long story short, we packed up his shop in Hollywood in a little over a week, moved over to Grenada, opened up a new shop, where Trick's other assistant, Mike, became the face of the shop that people interacted with, and we moved into the house beside it. We worked with the doors closed and ran anything that had to do with the outside world through Mike."

Looking around, I could tell they were each hanging onto every word I said, and a part of me felt good that they weren't kicking me out or running for the hills.

"I never saw my mom after that night when I was sixteen, or Jim since the day he showed up at Trick's old shop, but apparently, after my mom's dad passed away, whom I never even knew about or met before, she stood to inherit the millions he'd left her.

I didn't find this out until later, but right after her father died, she went to this lawyer, Mr. Fitzgerald, and pleaded with him to make sure all of her inheritance would go to me before Jim could spend it.

He told her that the only way to do that would be for her to die and leave most of it to me, almost like a joke, but from what he told me, she'd insisted. Wouldn't take no for an answer. He told her that if she was serious, she couldn't just cut Jim out of the will entirely because he could challenge it, but that if she left him a small percentage, he wouldn't be able to. So she did all the paperwork with Mr. Fitz, then drove herself right off a fucking bridge."

I sent the back of my hand up to wipe the tears off my face.

"Jim got about a million, I think, but as far as I was concerned, Fitz handled everything, even got me a new last name so I could actually start over, and with Trick insisting I take the opportunity, I left."

Looking back up, I finished, "I moved here and set up my shop. Spent every last dime I got from my mother getting everything exactly how I wanted it.

Trick tried to keep tabs on Jim for me, and last I heard, he'd gotten wrapped up in some mafia shit. Really, when I heard that, I thought that would be the end of Jim being in my life. But that was Mr. Fitz on the phone. He said Jim and some other guys broke into his office, held him at gunpoint, got my info out of his safe, and left, but then Jim obviously came back into the office and shot him. Jim picked up the phone, told me he'd see me soon, and called me a thief. Now we're here." Almost to myself, I added, "I guess it took him four and a half months to spend everything he got, too, and now he wants what I don't even have anymore."

The guys were silent for a while, sharing looks with one another as if they were having a conversation through sight alone.

When Diego got up a few minutes later and went into the kitchen, I stood up too.

"Now, I know you guys have your club and rules and

whatnot, but as you can probably tell, I really need to go," I said. "Jim could be on a plane right now, and who knows what kind of goons he's got with him. I need to grab what I can so I can leave. Go somewhere where he won't find me again."

Anchor stood up and walked over to me, slowly, gently, putting his hands on my biceps. "No. You don't need to run anymore."

"I don't have a choice," I said, nearly crying again.

"Yes, you do," Prowler said.

Looking as resolute as I think I'd ever seen someone look in all my life, Anchor said, "You're with us now. We're not going to let anything happen to you. I can promise you that."

"But really, guys," I pleaded, "Other than fixing the Panhead, you don't owe me. So why in the hell would you do anything for me? I mean, hell, I just met two of you today!" I'd pulled away from Anchor while I was talking, but none of their eyes left me as I moved.

Looking like a whole snack himself, Diego broke into what we were saying, distracting all of us. "Because we want to, and we can," he said all nonchalantly as if this were just a regular thing for him. "Now, everybody, get in here and get you some rice and tacos while they're still hot."

CHAPTER 8
Skye Sutton

A short time later, we were sitting around Diego's table, digging into the delicious food he'd made. There was still some tension in the air, but it wasn't nearly as bad as it'd been before we started eating.

I took another bite of his incredible Spanish rice, savoring every morsel as Chase asked, "We're gonna need our go-bags, aren't we?"

"Yeah," Anchor said, squeezing more lime juice over his taco.

Chase looked a little guilty. "I just have to throw a few things in, and mine'll be ready."

Without looking up from his plate, Prowler said, "Defeating the purpose of a go-bag in the first place."

Chase lifted his chin with a crooked smile and huffed through his nose once as Bronx spoke up. "Where are you stayin,' anyway?"

At first, I hadn't known he was talking to me, but once

everyone's eyes drifted over to mine, putting me on the spot, I answered, playing off the delay as if I were just trying to finish swallowing the food in my mouth before I responded.

"Above my shop. Why?"

"How much room do you have up there? I mean, I'm good with sleepin' on the floor if I have to, but if there's a couch to claim, I'm callin' dibs right now," Bronx said with a smile.

Looking at him funny, I said, "More space than I know what to do with," in a sarcastic tone, but then the rest of what he'd said registered in my brain, and I asked, "What?"

Chase propped his elbow on the table and put his chin on his palm as he had earlier. "You really are adorable when you're clueless."

"Watch your mouth, Pretty Boy, or I'll start taking your hard-earned points away," I said, pointing my taco in his direction, grinning as I rushed to my own defense, but in his, I really didn't know what they were on about.

Chase put his arms on the table in front of him and grinned hard at me, those hot as fuck dimples of his showing up out of nowhere. If I'd been standing, I would've been worried about tipping over - it was one of those smiles that made girls' knees weak, I swear.

Trying to hide a smile of his own, Anchor said, "We're gonna hang out at your place tonight. Or..." he paused for half a second, "until we know this problem with Jim is settled. We'd let you stay here for more protection, but you've got a lot of work ahead of you, prepping for the run that's coming up."

Huffing, eyebrows raising to my hairline in surprise, I looked at them like they'd all lost their minds. "When was this discussed? And no, the fuck you're not. None of you are," I said as I dropped my hands to my lap instead of picking up my taco again.

"When is she gonna get it that she doesn't have a choice here?" Chase asked everyone around the table, causing a smile to spread across my face despite myself and the position they were putting me in.

The rebellious, independent side of me wanted to lash out at them, put them in their place, and demand... something, but the more I considered it, the more I knew that having them stay with me made sense, so rather than biting back at him immediately, I sat there for a second, weighing my options.

I probably had enough time to get my shit together and go if that's what I chose to do because Jim and whoever he was working with were still back in Cali. At least for the time being. However, from the second Anchor said I didn't need to run anymore, that idea planted itself deep within me and sprung to life with incredible speed and intensity. The damn thing might as well have been in full bloom already, and I didn't want to rip it out. Ever.

To never have to run from Jim again? To start living my life without constantly looking over my shoulder and being hyper-vigilant about possible threats to my existence?

Gah, that sounded like a dream so sweet I could taste it.

One I craved, even.

If having these guys stay with me was the only way I

could see that dream through to the end, why would I dismiss it or shut it down like some random game of whack-a-mole?

In fact, it sounded to me like I was getting the better end of the bargain.

It might not have been pretty, flattering, or at all admirable, but I was more than willing to let these guys act as my bodyguards for the foreseeable future if it meant Jim wasn't going to be able to get to me.

Then again, though, was it really that selfish of me if they were the ones being so insistent? Was it not an even exchange for getting involved with this club and becoming their official mechanic in the first place?

"I have questions...," I said, still a little wary, which caused a round of small chuckles to meet my ears. "You're all coming? What about your duties or responsibilities or what-ever that you have here?"

"Yeah, we're all coming," Bronx said. "We're kind of a package deal, Sweetheart."

"If anything pops up with the club, we can handle it from your shop," Anchor said around a bite of food.

"Not trying to be a smartass or complain or anything, but did it ever even cross you guys' minds to ask me if you could spend the night rather than just inviting yourselves over without permission?"

Five no's, and a round of head shakes were their imme-diate responses as if they were five different versions of the same person or so intricately linked that they couldn't help but adopt some of each other's mannerisms. I rolled my eyes and smiled back, hardly containing the laughter that wanted to bubble up from inside my chest at how they'd answered in unison.

"Fine," I said, like I had any other choice. "You guys can stay with me."

Eyes and smiles were sent my way, but I ignored them and buried all the nerves I felt at the idea of having them in my space, deep inside my chest somewhere, as we finished eating. However, before I knew it, we were standing in the third-floor hallway, and each guy had a black duffle in hand.

They were ready to go, but as I started heading toward the staircase, Diego lightly put a hand on my shoulder, pulling me up short.

"Here, put this on," he said, handing me his cut.

Looking at it and only knowing what taking, accepting, and wearing that cut meant to the people of this club because of all the romance novels I'd read, my eyes grew wide as I looked up at him. "What? Why?"

He took a step closer to me, grinning confidently. "I want you to."

Huffing with an unintentional smile as butterflies erupted in my stomach, I said, "That's not a good enough reason," my voice coming out weaker and softer than it would have if I'd been telling the truth.

I knew my face was showing everything I was feeling despite what I'd said, refusing to cooperate and keep all that shit under wraps - as if I were an open book, screaming that, at least on some primal level, I did, in fact, want to be claimed by Diego... by all of them, if that were something that was even remotely possible.

Still, I wasn't about to say how much I wanted it out loud. Not in a million years. So I kept up my lying facade, even though I knew they probably saw right through it.

Smiling wildly at my reaction, he tried again. "How 'bout you wear it, so no one tries to grab that tight ass of yours again on the way out, and then none of us will have to get locked up for murder."

I closed my mouth on whatever I was about to say because my breath caught in my throat, and heat suddenly built up to a fever pitch, low in my belly.

"Fine, but this is the last thing you guys are gonna make me do while I'm here."

I'd been a little frustrated by how much I was signing up to do for the club already, but when all that got twisted up inside me with the lust-filled urges I felt every time one of these guys opened their mouth, things only got worse.

"When we get back to my shop, you're going to be on my turf, and there, everything is going to be on my terms," I said as I shrugged into Diego's cut, not letting myself snuggle into the warmth he'd left in it like I wanted to.

His patched leather hugged me when I pulled it tighter and looked down at my body, hair falling down around me as I took in the look of it combined with the ripped edges of my shorts, the stiff toes of my boots, and the grease stains on my legs.

I had to admit, it was hot, even to me.

"Got it?" I asked, raising my eyes back to look at the pack of men standing in a half circle around me.

To say I was caught off guard would've been an understatement.

All five stared me down with unbidden, ravenous desire written over each of their faces as the energy between us skyrocketed.

I could've fucking preened.

Instead, I savored every drop of this newfound power I now seemed to have over these men without questioning where it'd come from and turned around like I had every right in the world to wield it, marching down the stairs as they trailed behind me, acting my ass off, pretending that the way they were looking at me wasn't going straight to my head... and my vagina.

Heads turned, and mouths gaped as I led the way back out through the clubhouse wearing Diego's cut, and something about that just emboldened the fuck out of me - though I couldn't have explained why if I tried. It was heady, the rush of excitement that rolled beneath my skin in tingly waves, but I ignored it as best I could until we were finally back out front, standing on the porch.

"She's ridin' with me," Diego said like he was laying down the law for a crime that hadn't even been committed yet, as I turned to watch him and the rest of the guys walk past me to their bikes.

"This time," Chase quick-wittedly retorted as his eyes roamed over my body while he moved to straddle his bike.

Handing me the helmet I'd had when I'd rode up on the

Panhead that he'd procured out of seemingly nowhere, Diego climbed on his bike and said, "Hop on."

My lady parts were in absolutely no mood to argue with that. "Gladly," I said with a sexy grin in his direction as I sent my eyes up and down his frame where he sat on his bike, just like Chase had done to me before I climbed on, and he sparked the engine to life a second later.

Vibrations were sliding through me when Diego reached back, grabbed both of my hands in his, and pulled them around him, placing them low on his smooth stomach that I could feel through his thin white t-shirt. My chest was up against his back, adding to the contact high he was giving me.

Then he revved the engine and took off, shooting fire through my insides.

I must have actually been high on everything I felt because, by the time we made the second turn, I got real ballsy and decided to have a little more fun with this man while I could. It was late and dark out, so I also knew no one would be able to see what I was doing.

Slowly, so he wouldn't notice at first, I started sliding my hands down, pretending that I was just trying to settle into the ride and get comfortable; however, within no time, I was spreading my fingers over the tops of his thighs while my legs squeezed him tightly between mine.

Rubbing just hard enough for him to feel it through his jeans, I started teasing him, getting close to where I could tell his dick was reacting to my touch with every move I made, but never actually getting close enough to give him what he wanted as the wind and city whipped past us in a blur.

In his defense, he made it a good four or five miles before he couldn't take it anymore.

His left hand unbuttoned his jeans in a hurry, grabbed my wrist tightly, and sent my open palm into the hidden cavern of his jeans, right where he wanted it.

Immediately, I grabbed his hard length with my left hand and pulled his body tightly to me with my right, which was wrapped around his stomach. Then, practically salivating at his size, I started stroking him up and down as best I could from that angle and within the unforgiving confines of his jeans.

It was nowhere near enough satisfaction for either of us, but that didn't stop me. I kept going as I felt his breathing increase while he drove, his back pressing into my chest with each quickening breath he took.

It was hot as fuck, riling him up when I knew I would just let him down as soon as he pulled into my shop's parking lot a few moments later. So while it lasted, I worked him hard, moving in time with our rapid breathing, but when he parked, I stopped what I was doing and climbed off fast like nothing was going on at all when the rest of the guys parked too.

The two of us played it off well if I did say so myself.

We barely even acknowledged each other aside from a lightning-fast, intense dose of pointed eye contact when we took our helmets off, and he sat his in his lap, covering his open zipper. Then, grinning a little, I skipped off to the stairwell that led to the side entrance of my apartment, confident that the guys following behind me were none the wiser about what I'd just been doing to Diego.

Then, when I was at the top of the stairs, I unlocked the door, turned on the lights, and led a bunch of sexy, hot as fuck bikers into my home.

———

"I've got two guest bedrooms back there," I said, pointing behind me when I realized all the guys were standing there, wide-eyed like they didn't know where it was safe to walk, "but they're just empty rooms right now. I've also got these four couches that you can sleep on here."

"Just by breathin' in here, I'm gonna fuck this place up," Chase said, eyeing my apartment, barely moving.

"What? Why?" I couldn't help but ask.

His gaze moved to mine. "It's clean and fancy! Anything I touch is gonna get dirt on it."

Laughing at all of them because they looked like statues, remarkably out of place, standing off to the side of my living room, I said, "I'm a fucking motorcycle mechanic. I wouldn't have bought furniture that couldn't handle a little grease and grime. Come on in already. Come in." I used overexaggerated motions with my arms to show just how little I cared about what they were worrying themselves over. "Make yourselves at home; I promise, it's okay."

They moved toward me some, but after a few seconds, it was obvious they needed more assurances.

Grabbing the duffle out of Anchor's hand, I chucked it onto the couch closest to me. "You'll sleep there. That's your space. Have at it." Then, I walked over to Diego, pulled his bag from his grasp, and threw it at one of the other couches. "And that's yours. Do I need to do the same for the rest of you, or do you think you've got it?"

One of my hands landed on the hip I'd stuck out to the side as I eyed them.

Smirking at me, Anchor took the lead, which I was instantly grateful for, all the way up until the point that he was jumping over the back of the couch with his bag on it, crossing his legs over one another where they landed on his duffle and sent his hands behind his head - then I was a little ruffled.

I knew they'd take the track if I gave them an inch.

"You don't have to tell me twice. This is comfortable." His eyes were full of playful energy I hadn't seen in him before, so it lessened my ire as I spoke to him.

"You could at least keep your boots off the furniture, but I think that's probably a rule for anyone's house."

Smiling while he moved, he sat up and started unlacing his boots. "Just testing the waters, you know?"

"Uh-huh," I said as the rest of the guys started making their way around the space, and I turned on my heel. "I'm going to wash all this grease off. I'll be back in a bit."

"Can I come?" Chase asked.

I sent my gaze over my shoulder as I walked down the hallway, only answering him with a wink before I stepped into my room and couldn't see him anymore.

"Was that a yes?" I heard him ask, and I had to stifle the giggle that tore through me at his words.

"I have no idea." That was Prowler's voice; I was sure of it.

"I'm gonna take that as a yes."

I heard his booted feet walking toward me, and I couldn't help myself; I closed the door and locked it right as he came into view and laughed out loud when he said, "One day it'll be a yes; I can promise you that!" yelling like he wasn't close enough for me to hear him through the door. "And damn if I can't fucking wait for that day." His voice trailed off as he walked back to the living room, but I was just dying of hysterics over his flattery, so I didn't even say anything back.

A few beats later, I got myself under control, even if the smile on my face wouldn't go away for the life of me, and went about hopping in the shower.

It felt good to breathe again without any tension as the scalding hot water cascaded over my skin and through my hair. When I thought about it, I knew I should've still been freaking out about Mr. Fitz and Jim, but the guys in my living room had worked some kind of magic on me. I couldn't find the ability to worry about anything, and though I would've usually seen that as a red flag because that was always when the other shoe tended to drop in my past, something about these men had me feeling like something different was going on here.

"Fuck," I said out loud as realization dawned, and my movements stopped with the shock of it.

I actually felt *safe* with them.

Each and every one of them.

I couldn't...

My brain, it...

I had no words.

The only person I'd ever felt truly safe with in this entire world had been Trick, and here I was, barely knowing the guys who were spending the night with me, and I was one thousand percent sure nothing bad was going to happen to me while they were here.

My heart fluttered fast in my chest as I thought my palms started sweating, even while I was in the shower.

Taking an involuntary step to the side, placing my back up against the cold tile wall, I closed my eyes and breathed one of the deepest sighs of relief I thought I'd ever breathed in my life.

Surrounded by the stability I'd bought and implemented in my home and the security force now manning it, tears started falling out of my eyes with a vengeance all over again, but they were happy tears this time. Ones that fell because I was just so fucking ecstatic I didn't know what to do with myself; I knew that wasn't the right word, but no other description came as close to what I felt as that one did.

They knew all about my past and weren't judging me for it either.

It felt like finally being able to breathe again after being held underwater for so long your lungs burnt to a crisp inside your chest.

The flood of oxygen hitting each of your cells as you broke the surface?

The rush of, 'oh, you are going to live!' when you'd been so sure you were going to die?

That kind of relief hit me so hard it was like a tsunami of emotion spreading over me, through me, engulfing me - its presence threading the first healing stitches in the gaping lacerations on my soul, and I couldn't have been happier about it if I tried.

———

It took longer than I thought it would to pull myself together, finish getting ready in my pajamas, and head back out to the guys, but I got it done eventually, and I wasn't even hiccupping that much anymore by the time I walked into my living room.

Anchor, Chase, Prowler, and Brawler were all sitting on the floor around my square coffee table while Diego sat on the couch closest to me with his back facing me.

Without second guessing myself, I walked up and sat down close to Diego, but not so close that we were touching.

"What are you guys playing?" I asked, noticing they were knee-deep in some kind of card game.

"Spades. You wanna team up with Diego and play whoever wins?" Anchor asked, barely looking up from his cards.

Someone had some pretty good rock music playing through the speakers on their phone, where all their phones were laid on the table next to their pistols while they played the game, adding to the fun, laid-back atmosphere they were creating in my space.

However, when I sent my eyes to Diego to see what he thought about teaming up with me, I knew there was something entirely different on his mind as his gaze fell on mine. I could feel it. His lust-filled eyes sliding slowly down my body, leaving a trail of tingles on my skin everywhere he looked.

"Nah, I'm okay," I heard myself say without much thought.

Diego licked his lips, tilted his head slightly, then looked back at the game in front of us. Still, I could tell all of his awareness was on me, and only me, and mine was on him, even when I looked back at the game too.

Shifting, making it look like he was just trying to spread his legs a little wider, his knee brushed up against mine and stayed there, electricity sweeping through me at the contact.

"Why not?" Chase asked, drawing my unseeing eyes to his.

I answered, but again, all of my thoughts were on Diego and the subtle movement of his leg, rubbing up and down against mine. The movement was so small that no one could see it, I was sure, but damn if I didn't feel it in every part of me.

"I don't wanna."

I could've come up with a better answer than that, but really, I was just lucky my voice hadn't come out sounding all sultry and sinful, which were the only things I was really feeling at that moment.

Shifting my gaze back to Diego as the guys started arguing about something small that happened in the game, I sent him my most challenging glare because I couldn't hold back anymore. We were going to do something about all this tension, or I was going to explode.

He met my eyes and held them as he leaned forward and put his elbows on his knees. One of his hands went up to cup his chin, and it was all I could do to not melt when he looked at me like that.

Testing him again to see what he'd do, I said, "I need to go throw some stuff in the wash," and got up from the couch, knowing Diego's eyes were following me until I walked behind him.

Forcing myself to walk at a normal pace, barefoot on the hardwood floors, I was all too aware of the fact that my ass was practically hanging out of my sleep shorts and that the shoulder strap for this tank top had fallen off my shoulder too.

I walked through the frosted glass door that led to my laundry room, closed it behind me, and went to the dryer to turn it on, even though nothing was in there. A few seconds later, I'd barely turned back around when Diego walked in and put his back up against the door to close it.

Our eyes met instantly, and within the span of my next breath, we rushed each other, his lips meeting mine with so much passion-filled emotion I couldn't even think straight.

His hands gripped both sides of my face as our tongues

danced, and he spun me around so my back was now up against the frosted glass, his body pushing against mine, trapping me.

His kiss was everything I'd been hoping it would be since I met him a week ago. Honestly, I didn't think I'd gone an entire hour since then without his face popping up in my brain, and judging by how he was touching me now, I got the impression that he'd been doing the same with his thoughts of me.

Sending his knee forward, he got me to spread my feet apart, then he sent one of his hands from my face to cup everything I had down there with a hard, warm hand I ground against shamelessly.

Pulling back so he could look at me, his other hand reached up to grab me by my chin like he had earlier tonight.

Silly me, I had the same reaction now as I had then - the movement just made me smile wickedly.

"Do you know what I did tonight by claiming you in front of the club?" his voice was a husky whisper, causing even more wetness to seep out of me and into his hand in anticipation.

Smirking and dropping my hands to my sides limply to create more friction where I wanted it, I asked, "Do you know what I accepted when I put on your cut?"

He hadn't expected me to say that, and I knew it. Surprise raced across his features, then that surprise gave way to even more desire than he'd had before, delighting me to no end.

Diego sent his face up beside mine so he could whisper in my ear again.

"I made you mine. Do you understand?"

Fuck, I could've melted right there, but I had to keep my wits about me.

"No," I said, all breathy, "You made me yours, Anchor's, Prowler's, Bronx's, and Chase's." Each name I spoke had the heel of his hand grinding against my swollen clit with just the right amount of pressure to have me practically panting out their names as I said them.

He chuckled darkly at me, increasing my desire for him tenfold. "Damn straight." Pulling back again so he could look me in the eyes, he said, "You belong to all of us now."

I would've purred if I were a cat.

"But after that stunt you pulled on the way here, I will definitely be the first to have you."

I wanted to pant something like, 'uh-huh,' but didn't get it out of my mouth before he backed up a half step and ripped my shorts and thong down so fast I was hardly able to register the movement before he was reaching back up to pull my tank top off.

Standing there, bare before him, adrenaline raced through my veins as he took another step back, eyes roaming languidly over every inch of my skin as he took his sweet time unbuttoning his jeans for the second time tonight.

When he pulled his hard length out, I saw it twitch when I gave it my attention, and I sent my tongue out to lick my lips in response, a guttural sound coming from him a moment later.

Diego pulled a condom out of his wallet, dropped his wallet on the floor, ripped the foil open, and slid the thing down his length with fast, well-practiced movements, then just as fast, he came back over to me, resting his hard, heavy cock up against my belly.

His lips went to mine again, and I lost myself in his movements as he reached down and picked me up, so my knees were situated in the crux of each of his arms. He guided himself to my entrance, and without missing a beat or breaking our kiss for a second, he slid all the way inside me in one perfect go.

I moaned into his mouth, breathing hard, and as he started to move a moment later, he did the same, which sent me reeling.

Diego was stretching me, filling me entirely with each powerful thrust he made, setting me on edge, but when he dropped his forehead to mine and said, "Fuck, you feel so good," while he looked me in my eyes, I became liquid putty in his hands, moldable to his desire, and came all around him, biting my lip as a wave of absolute ecstasy flowed over me.

Never in my life had a man made me come so fast, from penetration alone at that, but I wasn't complaining one fucking bit.

His smirk nearly had me doing it all over again as he waited for the final waves of my orgasm to run their course, then slid out of me and set me back on my feet. He grabbed my hips, turned me around, and moved his foot between mine to get me to spread my legs again. Then, pushing me into the glass, the icy cold of it seeping into my nipples, making them even harder than they'd been before, he grabbed me by the hair and roughly pushed my face sideways up against the glass.

When he had me where he wanted me, he slid into me with so much force that I almost came again, but as I opened my eyes and saw the silhouette of someone standing on the other side of the door, panic surged through me.

However, I wasn't about to stop the pounding Diego was giving me, especially when the hand he wasn't using to hold onto my hair slapped my ass hard as fuck.

A cry tore through my throat; there was nothing I could do to stop it.

Whoever was standing in the hallway, watching me, added to everything I felt. Knowing one of the guys was getting a show tonight and imagining which one it could be, on my next breath, I came completely apart at the seams, wetness pouring out of me and around Diego before it dripped down my legs to land on the floor.

"Oh, you like being watched. Good girl," he said before that orgasm was totally finished, revitalizing it, so it rebounded and started all over again at his words, another wave of perfection tearing through me as a blissful, needy kind of whimper sounded through my lips.

"Fuck," he sent his face to my neck and growled out as he stilled, finding his own release deep inside me.

The man's silhouette walked off, heading back toward the living room, and more adrenaline coursed through me. Who had it been? Was he going to tell everyone in the living room what Diego and I had been up to? Were any of them going to be mad? Or would they not care at all?

I was positively freaking out on the inside, but all that worry was wiped away as Diego turned me around gently, lifted his hand to my chin slightly, and brought his dark lips to mine again.

This kiss was soft, sweet... fuck, it was perfect.

My hands landed on his sides as he kissed me, while both of his slid up my face and into my hair, gripping softly before he broke away and looked me in the eyes again, still holding me by my hair.

"That was exquisite, Baby Girl."

I couldn't think of anything better, so I smiled and said, "A hundred points to Diego."

He chuckled, sending his forehead to my shoulder for a second before he backed up and started cleaning himself up.

"Pretty sure I earned more than that. You came like three times."

Giggling to myself while I reached down to pick up my clothes so I could get dressed, I said, "I already told you; I don't come cheap. You're gonna have to work extra hard to get more points than that."

"Understood," he said, smirking that evil, cocky-ass grin at me that had my insides quivering every time I saw it.

When he'd adjusted his clothes and righted himself, he winked at me before he walked out of the laundry room, closing the door softly behind him, and once I was alone, I blew out a breath as an uncontrollable smile erupted across my face.

I knew I could stay locked up in this room, driving myself nuts with worry about what the guys were going to say to me when they saw me next, but I also wasn't ashamed of anything that'd just happened, so without further thought on the matter, I walked out, and made my way over to the couch to sit back down next to Diego.

In everyone's defense, no one said a thing to either of us as I brought my legs up on the couch and set my feet off to the side. Even when Diego sent an arm out and draped it around me, pulling me into his side while we watched the guys play spades, they kept their focus on the game.

Diego's hand rested on my thigh while I finally let myself snuggle into the warmth of his chest, his thumb moving slowly, back and forth softly across the bare skin I had there, drawing a contented yawn through my lips.

I must've had a long day because, within what felt like minutes, I drifted off to sleep on Diego's chest, reveling in some of the best feelings I'd ever felt in my life.

CHAPTER 9
Chase Evans - Cruiser

"Haha, she's knocked," I laughed quietly, so I wouldn't wake Skye up.

She'd passed out and was now laying with her head on Drifter's lap, looking properly fucked and happy, which only made me jealous by a fraction because she hadn't warmed up to me as fast as she had Drifter. She also seemed more peaceful and content than I'd seen her before this moment - when she was awake, she had a permanent I'm-ready-to-fight-anybody look about her, which was cute as fuck coming from her short, tiny ass frame, but seeing her like this was just as good.

"Yeah, but now I can't move," Drifter said, glancing down at Skye's sleeping face like she was a ticking time bomb that might go off if he moved.

Chuckling at that, I stood up to fix the problem. "I'll take her to her room. One of you go ahead of me and pull her covers back."

Prowler got up in my periphery while I leaned down and slid my hands under her head and knees. She didn't stir much, but when I lifted her up easily, she sent her face into my chest and an arm around my neck. Unable to hide the winning smile that formed on my mouth at that, I started carrying her down the hallway, rolling my steps so I wouldn't jostle her too much.

When I got to her room, I didn't want to just set her down and walk out, but I knew I had to so we could make a game plan before tomorrow.

Her bedroom was dark aside from where she'd left her ensuite bathroom light on, giving me enough light to see by so I could avoid walking on the giant, plush white rug she had in here. She had fancy purple sheets and a four-poster bed, giving me all kinds of exciting ideas when I saw them. After laying her down, I pulled the blankets over her and stood there for a second as I watched her get cozy in them, her long brown hair going every which way.

"Ten points to Chase," she mumbled sleepily as she rolled on her side, facing me, pulling a laugh out of my throat before I turned around and walked back to her living room.

I might not have known Drifter was gonna claim her as ours in front of the club tonight, but no one was gonna hear a peep out of me about it. She'd been impressing me with every move she made and every word she said since the day I met her, which was usually a hard thing for women to accomplish with me.

None of them had ever held my interest for too long

before I got bored and moved on, but Skye had been on my mind all week now, and I knew it would only get worse after everything we went through tonight. Something about her had just drawn me in, caught my eye, and wouldn't let go from when I saw her outside her shop, covered in paint. Then when she told us about her life, I couldn't help but want to protect her even more, regardless of how the club ended up weighing in on the matter.

Something about how the guys were treating her had me thinking we were all in the same boat in that regard, which was also surprising.

Granted, we'd shared women before, in different combinations - Prowler and I had both been with one while Anchor, Brawler, and Drifter were with someone else or different configurations like that... but we'd never claimed any of them because there had never been one that fit well with each of us at the same time.

However, it looked like things were going to be different with Skye.

Then again, I was also the eternally optimistic one of the bunch, so I had to take that idea with a grain of salt. I could never really predict what the guys would do when it came to their love life or who they were fucking, so for the time being, I was just gonna let things play out how they wanted to, fully intending on doing everything I could so at least I was able to be with Skye.

It was pushing midnight when I walked back into the living room and sat on the couch Drifter was on.

"Yeah, I want 'em on rotation between here and the

clubhouse twenty-four seven..." Anchor said, talking on his phone to the prez, I assumed. "There're enough prospects to get it done, even with their regular jobs."

"The prez?" I asked Prowler on the next couch over.

He nodded but never looked up. His gaze was locked on something on his phone, but that wasn't out of the ordinary for him, and we never gave him any shit about it unless we had to because we knew some wires were just switched in his brain. It'd always been like that for him since he was a kid.

I didn't think someone with a past like his *could* come out of what he'd been through and done without some kind of permanent damage to his psyche.

The carnage that man could inflict without any signs of remorse? The shit I'd seen him do when we let him loose? That kind of thing was only reserved for the worst of the worst, but it also had to happen from time to time, just so he wouldn't go crazy and lose it on the wrong people. So there was a delicate balance we had to keep up for him, and we did so gladly because we'd seen half the shit that had fucked him up in the first place and helped him bury the bodies.

"Alright," Anchor said before he hung up and cleared his throat.

Glancing between us as he spoke, he said, "The prospects are gonna be on protection detail between here and the clubhouse until we see this Jim thing through. Hopefully, it's just him that we're up against, but if he brings his mafia buddies with him, it's gonna be a whole different ball game we need to be ready for."

"I don't see why she never offed him before she came here," I said, throwing my feet up on the coffee table. "I mean, look at how tough this chick is. If anybody could've done something about him before now, I'd think it would've been her."

Prowler raised his eyes to me with a look that said I was missing something obvious.

I hated it when he did that.

"Oh, yeah," he said, his voice monotone, "because it was so easy for me to handle my dad way back when. It would've been even easier for a girl like Skye. She should've just done what we did instead of leaving. How weak of her." He rolled his eyes, sending a sickening feeling through my stomach at how right he was, and sent his gaze back to his phone. "And take your feet off her furniture."

"Sorry, man," was all I could get out before I moved my feet and rubbed a hand down my face as Drifter spoke up.

"I don't care who we have to merc. I'm invested," he said with a small laugh, lifting both hands up with a smirk.

"Now, we all are," Anchor said. "You told everyone at the club she was ours, so we're standin' behind you on that."

Huffing without humor, Drifter sat forward and put his elbows on his knees. "Oh, don't act like you're mad about it. We all know you better than that. You're into her too and happy about this arrangement; just admit it."

Drifter had always had a way with Anchor that made him stop being so fucking serious all the time, ripping him out of his big brother position every now and then, and this was one of those times. Anchor's smile lifted the corners of his mouth by a fraction of an inch, a dead giveaway that every word Drifter had said was right on the money.

A second later, he was back in that mode, though, looking between us as he said, "Speaking of which, before this goes any further, I think we need to vote on Skye."

My eyebrows raised as I looked around the room.

Nope, none of us were expecting that.

"Who here, other than Drifter, is plannin' on pursuin' her?"

I raised my hand immediately, thinking it was just gonna be me, Drifter, and Anchor raising our hands, but within half a second, every hand in the room was up, and my suspicions were confirmed.

"Alright," Anchor said. "Now, I need to know if any of you have a problem with this."

Every hand dropped as a smile of my own spread across my face.

"The ultimate decision will be up to her about who she wants to be with then." He leaned back, and if I wasn't mistaken, he almost looked worried. Did he not think Skye was into him too? Because I'd seen the way she was checking him out and smirking at him. Maybe he had a different impression.

My eyebrows had drawn down in the middle as I stared at him.

"What?" he asked me flat-out because the man had no filter sometimes.

Laughing, I poked at him with my words as I spoke to everyone but him. "Did you guys see Anchor's face a second ago? I think he's worried Skye won't want him, too." Then I laughed at just how preposterous that whole scenario was.

"Who are you to be laughin' at that? You're worried too, I can tell." Anchor was smiling with me, so there were definitely no hard feelings. "Plus, she said no to showering with you already tonight. If anyone here needs to be worried here, it's you, Pup."

"Man, don't call me that," I said as I laughed and threw a tiny decorative pillow at him.

He caught it good-naturedly and whipped it back at me.

A few seconds later, Prowler said, "There're four couches out here and a chair in her room, so somebody's sleepin' in that chair. Who's it gonna be tonight?"

"Me," I spoke up first, pulling groans out of all the guys, but it was a thing for us that we had to honor. Whoever spoke up first won, always.

Chuckling to myself, I got up and grabbed my bag, lifting a hand in the air as I started heading toward Skye's bedroom. "Night, fools! Sucks to be you!" I said, laughter following me in my wake.

Before long, I had the armchair in her room situated between the door and her bed. I sat down in it with my back to Skye, leaned my head against the chair, and closed my eyes, falling asleep quickly with Skye's little snore acting as my lullaby.

———

Disjointed images filled my mind while I slept when something touched my arm, and I startled awake, reaching for the pistol I had tucked in my waistband, my eyes opening wide as I started springing to my feet. However, I couldn't rise from the chair before Skye's yell hit my ears, and I froze mid-movement to assess what was happening.

"Jesus, fuck!" She jumped back nearly a foot at my reaction to being woken up.

It'd been such a cute reaction on her part that, as I tucked the pistol back in my jeans and forced myself to relax back in the armchair, I couldn't help but smile up at her shocked face.

"Nope," I said. "Not Jesus. I'm Chase, remember?"

That got her smiling at me again, which was a total win in my book.

"Why do you sleep with that so close to your junk? You're gonna blow your balls off one of these days." I could tell she was serious, but she was still smiling as she said it.

Standing up, I was surprised she didn't back up to allow me room, so I ended up about a foot away from her, looking down into her bright green eyes. "Are you worried about my balls? Because if you are, I'll let you check 'em out anytime."

She laughed outright at that, the sound making my dick grow harder than my morning wood had already made it. "You promise?" she asked, and I swear it jumped at what we were talking about.

Smiling, I closed the distance between us. "Anytime," I repeated, punctuating the word as I stood over her.

"Keep earning those points, Pretty Boy, and you might have yourself a deal." Her voice was low, nearly a whisper, as I got a whiff of her toothpaste that she'd obviously been awake long enough to use. She blinked at me with wide eyes, looking so innocently evil that I wanted to ravage her right there.

Leaning my head to the side a bit, I said, "Well, you gave me ten last night for carrying you in here. Then I sat by your bedside all night long, ready to off anyone who stepped through that door to harm you. I'd say I'm rackin' up points faster than you're lettin' me spend 'em."

Grinning as if she really liked my answer, she stepped forward, placed a hand on my chest as both of mine went to her curvy hips, and leaned her head back to see me better. I didn't dare move a muscle.

"Oh, I'll let you cash them in." Immediately, my whole body got excited. "You've just got to handle that morning breath first." She crushed my dreams as fast as she made them, but I stood steady, knowing she wasn't done. "Then again, by the time you're done with that, I'll already be in the kitchen making something to eat before I have to go to work."

Stepping back, grinning wildly because she thought she'd won this round, she said, "I guess that means you'll have to wait until I'm not busy to spend your points, and who knows how long it'll be until that time comes."

I didn't miss a beat.

"Lock the door."

"What?" she asked, like I had caught her off guard with that one.

Still smiling, I repeated myself, "Lock the door."

Eyeing me curiously with a smirk like no other, she never let her eyes leave mine as she walked over and did what I told her to, but then she stayed standing by the doorway, so I had to give her another directive.

"Get back over here."

She moved slowly, warily, but again, she did as she was told. It was taking everything I had in me not to move from where I was and rush her with all the pent-up desire I had for her, but because I could see how much she was getting out of being told what to do, I kept myself... mostly in check.

As soon as she stopped in front of me, I swooped her up, making her giggle and scream as I threw her onto the end of her bed, where her ass was right at the edge, and her legs were on either side of me.

I kneeled down on the floor and put my face between her thighs as she sat up on her elbows to look at me.

"You're not gonna smell my breath down here," I said as I sent my left hand to move her clothes out of the way, exposing all of her perfect, neatly trimmed pussy to me. "And I'm not waiting anymore."

She didn't tell me to stop.

In fact, her legs fell open even further to the side as her body did this little wiggle of anticipation thing, and she bit her lip.

Opening my mouth, I took her whole pussy in my

mouth and sucked, slowly dragging my tongue up through her folds, savoring how sweet she tasted as my eyes closed on their own for a second.

I lapped her up greedily over the next few minutes, her body twitching each and every time my tongue swept over her clit as I built her up and slowed down, built her up and slowed down.

When her soft moans sent her head back, and her hands gripped the bedding beneath her, I started going faster and faster, not giving her a moment's reprieve. I sent my right hand up to start fingering her while I worked her clit over with my tongue in a frenzy of motion, causing her whole body to start shaking.

She reached out and grabbed a handful of my hair as she squirted in my mouth and whisper-yelled my name.

I absolutely loved the fact that she was a squirter, but I didn't have a chance to bask in that for long before she pulled me up her body by my hair, while I wiped my mouth with my hand.

"Get inside me, now."

She didn't have to tell me twice; I was hard as fuck from eating her pussy and couldn't wait to do exactly what she wanted. Reaching into my jeans, I pulled out my wallet to grab a rubber, only to remember I'd used my last one a few weeks back on some chick at the club. I wanted to punch myself in the dick for not putting one back in there as soon as I met Skye, just in case.

"I don't have a condom."

Her face returned to that I'm-gonna-fight-somebody look I was growing used to seeing, and I was sure I'd just ruined this whole experience, but her words ended up making everything better.

"Then you're only half paid back." Then she smiled, and my heart started racing even faster than it'd been going before. "And I expect a redo soon."

"Yes, ma'am," I said as I stood up and sent a hand out to her to help her up.

She knocked it away with a small laugh and climbed off the bed, staring up at me a moment later with a wicked grin that made me nervous.

"I would like to cash in the favor you owe me now."

"Anything for you, Sweets," I chuckled. "What can I do for you?"

"Since you messed up my schedule by being so impatient, now I don't have time to make myself a good breakfast before I have to open the shop. I'd like for you to make it for me while I get ready, please. I think it's only fair."

This woman was fucking perfect.

"You got it." I smiled at her. "Now, go get ready."

She nodded and turned on her heel, looking quite content with herself before I reached out and slapped her ass, causing her to smile at me over her shoulder as she walked toward her bathroom.

"Couldn't help myself," I said, raising both hands in the air, which made her laugh again as I turned around and started heading toward the kitchen. If I had my way, I would enlist every man in this apartment to help me whip up a breakfast to die for, so long as she had what we'd need without going to the store.

Instantly, I knew this whole thing with Skye was so much better than anything else I'd ever experienced before, and damn if I wasn't completely fucking ecstatic about it.

CHAPTER 10
Skye Sutton

"So are you guys gonna pay me or what?" I asked everyone at once as we sat around my kitchen table and dug into what was essentially an entire breakfast buffet the guys had made.

I knew they had to have used up all the ingredients that were supposed to last me a couple of weeks in one meal, but with how good everything looked and tasted, I wasn't too upset by it. I just knew I was going to have to make another grocery run soon, which had been what sparked my question in the first place.

Laughing, Chase said, "You were paid before you even got up to Diego's room at the clubhouse last night."

I glanced at him with a disbelieving glare as I swallowed a bite of my eggs.

"Are you high? Nobody paid me anything." I sent my fork out to all of them to accentuate my point as I asked, "You know me being dubbed your official mechanic doesn't equate to dollar signs, right? And a girl's gotta eat, obviously." I sent my fork back to my plate, stabbed it into a piece of smoked sausage, and threw it in my mouth to further prove my point.

Smiling, Anchor said, "Check your account."

Sitting back in surprise, I grabbed my phone from the back pocket of my jean shorts and logged into my bank's app. Sure as shit, fifteen thousand, four-hundred eighty-seven dollars and sixty-two cents were sitting pretty in my account.

Still, I couldn't get past the fact that I had never given them any of the information they would've needed to put money in there, much less that staggering amount. Hell, I hadn't even told them what bank I was using.

"We're good at what we do, and Reaper said to put you on retainer. I figured that would be good enough to start with, but we can add to it if you need more," Chase said as I glanced down at his treasurer tab.

"It's more than enough. It's too much," I said, but I might as well have been talking to a room full of brick walls for all the good my complaint did in changing anything.

They all brushed me and my concerns off as if I didn't have any, and though it grated against my nerves that they knew so much about me, I would've been lying if I said it didn't also set me at ease somehow in this weird, twisted way. Even if I couldn't exactly explain my reasoning, even to myself.

When we were all done eating, laughing at a story Anchor told about Reaper getting stuck in a ditch somewhere, Prowler got up and started clearing his spot at the table, prompting all of us to do the same. I went to put my plate in the dishwasher, but he took it from me before I could get it in there. I wasn't going to argue, but as everyone else crowded around the island, talking and joking with each other, I took a step back and watched how Prowler was acting.

He was like a robot with a singular focus all of a sudden, cleaning up the entire kitchen fast and efficiently, never even looking up at anyone while he moved or adding to what the guys were saying like he'd been doing while we were at the table. Everyone else was standing nearby, but I could tell they were intentionally staying out of his way.

I had one hip leaning up against the cabinet in front of the sink where I stored the dishwasher tabs, and when he got to the point in his rigid cleaning where he needed them, he walked over to me and almost looked surprised to see me standing there.

His eyes only met mine for a second before I moved out of his way slowly, but in that second, I couldn't help but notice how lost he'd just looked. How worried his eyes had been. It made me want to reach out and hug him or something. Grab him by the shoulders and ask if he was okay, especially after how he'd helped me last night.

Someone laying a hand on my arm was the only reason I didn't.

The guys' conversation didn't skip a single beat as Anchor's gaze met mine. He shook his head slightly, almost in warning, even though he was still laughing and responding when it was necessary for the conversation.

It almost felt like they were keeping their spirits high on purpose, all while Anchor was obviously trying to warn me away from Prowler for some reason.

I backed up with the startling realization that they might have known everything about me already, but I definitely didn't know much about them, and instantly, self-deprecating thoughts started scrolling through the forefront of my mind, calling me out for giving away too much too soon to a bunch of men I didn't even know.

Now, granted, I would never apologize or feel bad for getting intimate with people when I wanted to, and they did too, so I wasn't worried about either of the sexual situations we'd had so far.

I was actually pretty freakin' happy about those.

But the emotional shit? Everything I'd told them last night at the club? Showing off all my weaknesses in one go with that fucking panic attack of mine too?

I'd gone entirely too far.

However, they hadn't exactly given me a choice; I argued with myself in my head. I hadn't thought I could do anything *but* share my past with them and answer their questions after that phone call from Fitz.

Then again, I thought, just because I hadn't learned much about them didn't mean I couldn't if I put my mind to it, and as I stood there, watching them, that task shot up to the top of my list. I was going to dive as deep into each of them as they'd let me go.

I just had to hope they wouldn't shut me out like that

voice inside my head told me they would as I finished getting ready for work.

A short time later, I was unlocking the front door of my shop, the guys trailing behind me, when more bikes than I could count from my angle started pulling into my parking lot. Walking through the door, making sure to stay back so I wouldn't be in the way, I watched as every parking space was suddenly filling up fast, with more starting to form a line out in the road, waiting to fill up the unmarked parts too.

Glancing back over my shoulder at a smiling Bronx, who was standing right behind me, I asked, "There's something wrong with all of them?" with my eyes going wide.

Chuckling smartly, he said, "Nah, most of 'em run at least, but we want 'em decked out. Your sign says customization. You can do that, right?"

"Of course I can." I swept my gaze back to watch all the commotion but quickly turned my head toward Anchor on my left and asked, "You want all of these fixed and outfitted by when?"

"The run is two months away to the day," he said, grinning like an idiot. Gah, I loved that smile, but I still wanted to pretend to be mad, so I stopped looking at him and sent my hands to my hips. "Don't worry, though; you'll have us and the prospects to help as much as we can."

Huffing through my nose with a dark chuckle, I said, "I'm definitely going to need it. What is this? Your whole fucking club?"

Laughing, he said, "This isn't even half of our Wilmington chapter, Babe. These are just the ones we decided needed the most work before the run."

Who was I kidding? I was pumped and couldn't help the smile I sent Anchor as those words came out of his mouth. Shocking me even more, it was like my smile had surprised him too, and in response, he sent a gentle hand up to my face to move a wayward strand of my hair back behind my ear.

Could my heart flutter any faster? I didn't think so.

When he dropped his hand back to his side a moment later, and I took a good look around, motivation like I hadn't felt since I moved out here, settling in me quickly and sending me straight into boss mode as if I had every right to do so.

I went back inside, grabbed an entire pack of tags with strings on them, a few notepads, and pens, unlocked and opened the garage door, then stepped back out, gesturing for the guys to come over to me.

"Alright, the only way this is going to work is if I know exactly what each bike and her biker wants and needs," I said as I opened the bag, handed a few tags, a notepad, and a pen to each of the guys, then took some for myself as well. "So we're going to treat this like some kind of mass casualty event, and we're the medics."

Smiles, concerned looks, and outright lust shined on the faces staring back at me, but I forced myself not to lose focus as I spoke to them.

"You're going to go to each bike in this lot, and those out there, parked on the street, and write down everything you can about it. If they need parts, I need 'em listed on that tag. If they need paint, I want a description of the design they want and a list of colors to go with it."

Pausing for a second as a concern raced through my mind, I asked, "And how are all these men getting back? Are they just going to walk or something?"

Anchor was the one to answer me. "We've got a couple of vans coming that are gonna act like shuttles to get them where they need to go. Don't worry."

"Perfect," I nodded. "For every tag that you make and hang on a bike, you're gonna make a note on that pad, so none of these ladies get lost in the chaos. Now, where are those prospects you were talking about, and how long can they stay and help out?"

"You can have 'em every day for the next two months. They were going to be here on protection detail anyway." I couldn't even attempt to analyze that just yet. "Prospects!" Anchor's voice boomed out of his throat impressively. "Line up on Skye!"

Immediately, eight men started running over to us, forming a line that stood shoulder to shoulder with each other, and I wasn't gonna lie - I was getting a kick out of all this, there was no doubt about it.

"Hey," I said once I had their attention. "I'm Skye."

"She's ours," Anchor said pointedly, interrupting me, but when I heard what he said next, I wasn't bothered by it anymore because I knew it had to be said in this crowd. "You will do everything she says as if one of us told you to do it. You will treat her exactly like she's one of us. Fail to do so, and you can say goodbye to ever getting your patch, do you understand?"

"Uh ah! Uh ah! Uh ah!" they yelled like everyone had last night in the club, and again, I had to stop myself from startling. Finally, however, I quickly pulled myself together and returned to delegating.

"You all are gonna be my gophers, my muscle, my extra set of hands, whatever I need at the time. Some of you will be on certain tasks I give you, and others might be waiting around for something to do. Either way, I want you within earshot if I need you."

Thinking quickly, I added, "It seems like you're going to be working here for the next two months, so you're going to treat this like a job you really want, okay?"

"Uh ah! Uh..." I waved both of my filled hands through the air wildly with a disgusted look on my face.

"Fucking stop," I said, laughing a beat later as laughter erupted all around me. "Just nod or something, fuck."

Everyone was laughing for a second but sobered as I got back to what I was saying.

"The day starts when the shop opens at ten every weekday. I'm closed on the weekends. You'll have three breaks each day. Thirty minutes for lunch and two fifteen-minute breaks to use for whatever you want, and yes, you can combine those for a thirty-minute one if you'd like."

Head nods and smiles met me, so I finished up. "I only have three rules. Don't get high or use any kind of drugs while you're on this property, don't aggravate or piss off my neighbors, and if you have any problems whatsoever, come to me immediately." They all nodded again. "I'll pay you for your time here…"

Anchor cut me off. "No, the club will pay you."

Rolling my eyes, deciding that, too, was a discussion for another time, I said, "What he said might change, but for now, everyone head in the shop and wait for us to triage this lot."

Without waiting for another word, all the prospects started walking through my open garage door as I turned to my guys. "Alright, then," I smiled with a deep breath, "Let's get to work."

———

"Don't you guys already have day jobs?" I asked the prospect that had been 'assigned' to shadow me by Anchor as soon as we started working. I was pretty sure he said his name was Emry.

The blonde guy, who couldn't have been much older than twenty-one, laughed. "Those of us that do are at them right now."

Standing up from where I'd been crouched down, checking out a dent in one of the girls' frames, I laughed as I said, "Oh, so you guys are the ones who still live at home with your mamas."

Emry smiled good-naturedly at me as he answered. "No, we're stayin' at the club for a lot of different reasons, but mostly 'cause our mamas suck."

A haughty giggle bubbled through me. "Then I'm with the right club, that's for sure."

Changing the subject quickly, I said, "Alright, I think we're done here. Let's head back inside and get these babies sorted out."

When we got back inside, all of my guys were standing around the low table I had in the waiting area where each of their notepads were lying. Picking them up one by one, I started reading through every bike they'd listed to see what I was up against.

"Who's pad of what-the-fuck is this?" Laughter met my ears like they'd been half expecting me to say something about it, but I didn't look up. "And who in the hell taught you how to write like this? They need to be put away for child abuse."

"It's mine," Chase said. "Look, I don't have the best handwriting. This would've been much easier if I could've just texted it to you."

Chuckling, I said, "I think you're gonna have to; there's no way I'm figuring this out."

Dramatically leaning up against the counter, crossing one foot over the other with a cocky as fuck grin on his face, he asked, "So can I get your number? You know, so I can rewrite all that?"

I tossed his notepad over at him with a huff. "If you can send thousands of dollars to my bank account without asking my permission, I know you already have my number in your phone." I didn't know that for sure, but I had a feeling.

"We all do," he said as he smiled like the devil he was, getting me all hot and bothered again, thinking about this morning. I couldn't bring myself to do anything but smile at him before we all got back to work on the bikes a short time later.

To my shock and awe, things actually went really well for the rest of the day, and by the time five o'clock rolled around, we'd already knocked seven bikes off my to-do list - they'd only needed a few quick things, so we handled them first. The guys were super helpful all day. Hell, even the prospects seemed to be enjoying themselves while they worked cleaning parts, moving bikes around, or helping change a few tires.

Since everything had been going so smoothly, I should've known the other shoe was gonna drop soon. However, unfortunately for me, that shoe happened to be in the shape of my stepfather Jim and a slew of other suited men who walked up to my garage door like they owned the place instead of me.

It was everything I could do not to run in the other direction, but as my guys stepped between the suited men and me, and the prospects lined up at my back, I didn't think I could've run, even if I wanted to.

CHAPTER 11
Augustine Livingston - Anchor

Seven men in trim, tailored suits pulled up in two blacked-out Cadillacs, got out, and walked up to stand across from us in Skye's parking lot. All I could see in my head when I looked them up and down was that they were trying their damndest to seem like modern-day Peaky Blinders or something.

They weren't failing terribly at that, but they weren't in sync like we were either - I didn't need to tell my brothers what to do or where to move; they just stepped into place silently, readying themselves for whatever this turned out to be.

"That's her," one of the men said as they approached, pointing to Skye with an accomplished, satisfied smile on his face, which had the guy in the middle nodding his head once.

"Hello," the man in the middle spoke directly to me, then looked down at my patch, squinted his eyes dramatically, and said, "Vice President of the..." he paused, glancing around to everyone behind me, then added, "whatever this little club is that you have here," with a dismissive wave of his hand.

"We'd like to speak to that one," he knife-handed Skye, "but since she's hiding behind all of you big bad biker men like a scared little bunny, I guess we're going to have to talk first."

Forcing a fake laugh and putting a pompous-assed hand up over his heart a moment later, he said, "Sorry, I forgot I was in the south, and manners matter to you people. Please, excuse me. I'm Carl Capriotti, and this is some of my family." He slid both of his hands out to either side, indicating the men around him. "We flew all the way out here from California last night just to have a nice little chat with her, so if you would please be so kind as to send the little rabbit forward, my family and I? We would greatly appreciate it."

I could feel anger and aggression seeping out of each of the guys behind me, but they knew to stay where they were until it was go time.

"Well, your 'manners' could use a lesson in Heathen hospitality," I said, "but we can get to that later." Hooking my thumbs in my back pockets so my hands were closer to the gun I had in my waistband, I said, "You've got something to say, so say it; she's standing right there." I nodded my head back behind me.

Pursing his lips, Carl breathed through his nose before he took a step to his left so he could see her past me. "We have some business to discuss." He waited for a few seconds, but Skye didn't say anything, so he continued. "It seems there was a mix-up in some paperwork a few months back, and somehow you inherited a pretty substantial amount of money that wasn't meant for you."

Again, he paused, but Skye stayed silent. I wanted to turn around and see if she was okay, but I knew I couldn't take my eyes off of these guys.

"Stop eyeing me, you little cunt," the guy who'd pointed Skye out said, drawing my eyes to his, where they were locked on someone behind me. It didn't take a rocket scientist to know this was Jim and that he was talking to Skye. "Get your ass over here and quit playin' games."

"Did I say you could speak?" I asked, angling my head his way, but Carl spoke up, distracting me from Jim.

Sliding his hands all the way in his pockets and leaning forward some as he spoke, he said quietly, "This really is a family matter. We should let them work it out."

Jim didn't wait for Carl to finish speaking or acknowledge what I'd said before he opened his slimy ass mouth again. "You're going to give me every dime your bitch of a mother stole from me, and you're gonna smile while you do it. Now, don't make me tell you again, Missy. Get over here!"

"She's not going anywhere," Brawler said lowly from my right, smiling as he took a step toward Jim with the confidence only a life like his would've given him.

I was already calculating how this might play out - who'd move where, how fast they would pull their weapons, which of them to take out first... that kind of thing, but then, Jim's vitriol turned on Brawler.

"You stay out of this. I don't care whose dick she's been suckin.' This doesn't have anything to do with you, boy," and I didn't need to wonder why he hadn't spoken to me like that, the racist piece of shit.

Prowler moved subtly on my left, slow enough that Carl and the other mafia guys didn't notice - they were too caught up watching Jim. There was no telling what his plan was, but I trusted him and was more than willing to go along with whatever he was about to do.

Turning his gaze back to Skye, unaware of Prowler's movements, Jim said, "Is this what my money bought? A shithook bike shop and a bunch of dicks to sink your dry ass cunt on? You know, you don't just look like your mom, you fuckin act like..."

Pop. Pop. Pop. Three shots rang out in quick succession before I could even blink, and Jim fell to the ground, all three landing center mass as Skye walked into my line of sight and past me, firing the whole time.

Pop. She sent another round into his lifeless body, right into his face.

Then another, and another, and another.

At first, no one on the mafia's side moved, but we did.

By the time Skye had emptied the mag into Jim's body and was standing over him, looking down at his corpse without an emotion in sight on her face, me and all of my men had our guns trained on the remaining mafia guys, just waiting for them to step out of line.

"Well, that was unexpected, Little Bunny." Carl's tone had changed to one of bored annoyance, looking like he couldn't care less about the fact that Jim was dead and my pistol was trained on his cheekbone.

Rubbing his palms together as Skye looked back up at him, he said, "Losing Jim is an inconvenience, but not one we can't look past. However, the money you owed him? Well, that was money that he owed us, you see, and now his debt has definitely fallen to you."

Lowering my pistol enough to deal some damage but not outright kill him, I said, "His debt died with him," and pulled the trigger, lodging a bullet in his thigh.

Carl fell to the ground, gripping his leg, displaying a vast range of knowledge on how to use the word 'fuck' in a sentence, all the while screaming and wailing about how he was the son of an Italian mafia don and how this was not going to fly, and how dare we, and how this wasn't over, or some other such bullshit.

Raising my pistol to who I assumed was the next highest guy in charge, I said, "Take your boss and that dead ass piece of shit over there and get the fuck out of our city. Skye doesn't owe you or your family anything. No one on this coast does. And if I so much as hear of one you sneezing east of the Mississippi, you're all gonna end up like Jim here. Got it?"

Mafia dude number two nodded profusely while ignoring his boss's directives, which were telling him to do anything but what I'd just said, and got each of his men to start dragging Carl and Jim back to their Cadillacs. Surprisingly enough, it didn't take them longer than two minutes to tear out of here, tires screeching on the pavement as they drove off, but I knew by looking at Skye's face that it would take a while for her to process what had just happened.

In that way, she kind of reminded me of how Prowler could sometimes get lost in his own internal monologue because it was so much louder than everything else going on around him.

"I guess this means I don't have to teach you how to shoot?" Cruiser asked, trying to lighten the mood, but Skye didn't even respond. Her eyes had settled on the big red pool of blood on the ground outside her garage doors, and honestly, I wasn't convinced she'd even heard him in the first place.

"How did no one see or hear that?" Emry asked, his eyes wide with wonder as he looked both ways down the street, which was actually pretty empty for this time of day by some stroke of luck. Then, seeming to forget about that entirely, he turned to us and the other prospects.

"Did you see Skye? She was like a real-life Wynona Earp or something; just bam! Bam!" I could tell he wanted to keep going, but Skye moved over to him, shoved the empty gun she was holding into his chest sideways without looking at him, and started zombie-walking back into her shop.

"Did I say something wrong?" Emry asked, but no one answered him.

Walking over to him, I punched him right in the jaw.

"Don't you ever let someone take your gun off you again, do you understand me? Especially her. Who knows what could've just happened because you weren't paying attention."

Holding his right hand over his face, Emry smirked at me. "You told us to treat her like we'd treat you, Anchor, and there's no way I would've kept you from getting my gun if you needed it."

Damnit, that kid. I swear.

Chuckling, I sent a hand out to his back as he threw one of his on mine.

"This is gonna be a tough night," Prowler said, his eyes never leaving the door at the back of the shop that Skye had disappeared through.

"Fuck that," Brawler said. "It's gonna be a tough life."

"Why's that?" Emry asked.

"Because after this? Me shooting a mafia don's son in the leg? We're gonna be goin' to war for her."

CHAPTER 12

Princeton Avery - Prowler

I knocked on the door Skye had gone through, but there was no answer, so I slowly slid it open and looked inside.

The whole floor was covered with some kind of gray plastic stuff taped to the baseboards around the room. Four tall windows showed the moonlit harbor in all its glory while painting supplies littered the space everywhere I looked. To be as organized and clean as she was throughout the rest of this place, I could tell that she didn't care about cleaning up here. Dried splotches of different colored paint dotted the plastic on the floor as I walked over to her, but I could only focus on her standing statue still, staring at a blank canvas in front of her.

"Skye," I said hesitantly, but she didn't answer me.

Getting as close as I felt I could, I walked up beside her easel, watching as her bright green eyes veered over to mine.

"I'm fine," she said, her voice monotone, matching the emotionless expression she was sending me.

Trying to distract her in any way I could, I said, "You're a liar, Little Warrior."

She blinked twice at me, then sent her eyes back to the canvas.

"If you want to paint, you can," I said, "but you've gotta get the blood off first. There can't be any evidence left behind that could lead anyone to you."

Her eyes shot over at me with confusion before she looked down at her right hand, then further down her legs to her boots.

Blood splatter was all over her, even on her face, but I was going to do everything in my power to make sure she didn't see that part if I could help it.

"Will you come with me and let us get you cleaned up?"

"I didn't even recognize him when I was done." She'd started staring at her hand again without moving. "Like the bullets just..." she paused for a second, "tore his face apart."

I mean, I would've thought that was a good thing, but there was no telling where her emotions had her landing on that topic just yet.

She could've been seeing herself as some kind of monster. Or it could go the opposite direction and build her up on the inside. There was just no way for me to know how she felt until she said something else.

"He had no face." Her eyes went wide and unbelieving.

Yep, that was the bad path.

"Come on, let's head upstairs and clean you up." Reaching out to nudge her gently, thankful as fuck that she was allowing me to touch her right now, I got her feet to start moving, but she never lowered her hand from where she was holding it in front of her, staring down at the limb like she couldn't recognize it.

I figured her moving at all was as good a sign as I was going to get, and I started guiding her back through the garage to another door that had a staircase in it, motioning for the guys with my other hand.

"Get all this cleaned up and locked up. Holler if you need us," I heard Anchor say to the prospects before he and the rest of the guys from our crew started climbing up the steps behind us.

When we got into her apartment, she dropped her hand and started watching where she was going, which I also took as a good sign... up until the moment when she started running toward the kitchen, and I had to rush to keep up with her. Luckily, she made it to the trash can, but I mean, she only made it by half a second, if that.

I pulled her hair back as she retched, the rest of the guys standing nearby, wondering what to do, I assumed, because I was wondering the same thing.

"You all know I..." her words were cut off by another heave of her stomach. "Ugh," she groaned. "This is terrible."

"It'll get better soon, I promise," Drifter said. "This kind of thing happens to a lot of people the first time they take somebody out."

A few minutes passed, and she didn't seem like she would throw up anymore, so I pulled on her a little to get her to come with me. "Let's get you in the shower, okay?"

She nodded but kept her mouth closed as we started moving. However, when we were standing in her bathroom with the hot water running, she surprised me by saying, "Can you close the door, please?"

"Sure thing," I said, but as I began to step out of the bathroom to give her some privacy, she spoke up again, panic lacing her tone.

"No, don't leave, please." Her eyes closed for a second. "Just... just close the door."

Nodding, I closed it on the guys posted up in different areas of Skye's bedroom and walked back over to her.

"You don't mind me being in here?"

She shook her head again but didn't look up at me.

"Alright," I said, "I'll be right here," as I pushed my hands in my pockets.

"Okay." She turned away from me and started taking her clothes off.

Conflicting feelings were tearing through me, but I wouldn't acknowledge them. I was going to do whatever she needed me to do, and no, I couldn't justify why I felt this way. Why I cared so damn much. The point was that I did, and there wasn't any changing that.

When she climbed in a moment later, I reached down, picked up everything she'd been wearing, including her boots, and said, "I'm just gonna give these to the guys, okay?"

She nodded, the glass shower door wide open as she stepped under the water.

I took all the clothes to the door, handed them off to Drifter, who'd been standing the closest, then shut the door again. She'd scrubbed her face and gotten her hair wet by the time I got back over to her, but she was still nowhere near her normal self just yet.

Water was getting everywhere outside her shower, but I didn't think either of us cared.

Moving slowly, she grabbed a loofah that was hanging on the wall, poured some good-smelling body wash on it, then put the bottle back with a sigh. When she started scrubbing the red circles of dried blood off her hand, something changed, though.

Her face contorted. Her body leaned forward. She started scrubbing at her skin with that thing harder and harder and harder still, a harsh sound coming from deep inside her chest to pour through gritted teeth as she rubbed her skin raw with effort in an almost frenzied kind of panic.

I took a step toward her, intent on saying... something, but her movements slowed to a stop then, and she dropped the loofah.

The first ragged breaths in a long string of them caused her body to cave in on itself even further, powerful sobs wracking her entire body a moment later. Collapsing to her knees as she put her face in her hands, her heart-wrenching, audible sobs finally sparked me into action.

I couldn't just stand there.

I kicked off my boots and took my cut off, then climbed in beside her, stepping around her crumbled frame until I was in front of her, then sunk down and sat on the floor, pulling her into my chest a half-second later.

Water was drenching both of us, but I didn't care.

"Shhh," I said. "I know. It's over."

I rubbed her arm with one hand and her hair with the other as I started rocking her back and forth.

"He's gone now. You're *free*."

Pulling back and lifting her chin so she would look at me, I met her raw, red eyes with mine. "And you're the one that made that happen."

Looking confused and absolutely wrecked on the inside, I could see the wheels turning in her mind as she processed the fact that this was a good thing for the first time since she shot him.

"He's never going to hurt anyone else again, and you did that."

A glimmer of strength shimmered in her eyes for a brief moment.

"You bought your own freedom, and I'm so proud of you for that. You know that, right? Nobody else was doing anything, but you didn't wait. You just handled it. Now the whole world's a better place because he's not in it. Do you hear me?"

She nodded, but when more sobs continued to pour out of her, I wasn't upset.

Wounds as deep as hers were complicated and messy as fuck. They weren't just going to scab over and heal because the person who'd made them wasn't breathing anymore.

No. They took their sweet ass time to heal, and in my experience, a million sob-filled showers, at least.

There was nothing any of us could do to speed up the process, either. So we just had to wait patiently and ride the currents as they came, no matter how long they lasted, and I didn't care if I stayed in this shower with her until we were both freezing our asses off; I wasn't going anywhere.

CHAPTER 13
Diego Melendez - Drifter

Anchor's phone was lying on the square coffee table between us, ringing on speaker as we all waited for Reaper to pick up.

"Yeah," he answered three rings in.

"You got a second, prez?" Anchor asked. "We've got to tell you something."

"Hold on." He was obviously in the main room of the clubhouse, where loud music and people partying could be heard in the background. A moment later, things grew quiet on his end, and he turned his attention to Anchor. "Alright. What's up?"

Between Anchor and the rest of us, we filled him in on everything that had gone down from the moment we went up to Diego's room to now. He didn't say much while we talked, but that was just how Reaper was. He'd listen to everything, think about it for half a second, then start asking questions and dishing out consequences as he saw fit.

"The Capriotti Mafia out of California?" he asked.

"Yeah," Anchor replied.

Reaper was silent for a few moments, then asked, "How did our background check miss all this money shit with Skye? It should've been there to give us a head's up that this could be a potential problem."

We shared glances around the table at each other, but Chase was the one to answer him. "I'm assuming she used some of the money she got to buy people's silence. I mean, we haven't asked her or confirmed anything yet, but the people at City Hall were tight-lipped when we asked about her, and we couldn't find anything substantial on her before her move into Wilmington. If she paid people off and had that lawyer make more than just a fake ID and social, that could explain it."

"Smart girl," Reaper said, almost to himself, causing a smirk to settle on my face as I thought about her. "Well, at least we know she's a good shot," he said with a dark chuckle.

Agreements sounded around the table.

"Where is she now?"

"Prowler's in her room with her, getting her cleaned up," Brawler said. "She's not taking it that great, but Prowler seems to have a way with her, so hopefully, he can pull her out before she sinks too deep."

Brushing Brawler's concerns off, Reaper said, "Ehh, that girl's got more balls than half the men in this club; I'm sure she'll be fine in no time."

We all laughed at that for a second.

Putting my elbows on my knees, I leaned forward so he could hear me.

"How do you want us to handle this, Reap? The Capriottis aren't just gonna let this kind of thing slide."

"Well, boys, that depends entirely on how serious you all are on Skye. If she's disposable, we can make amends; if not, you know this means we're gonna have a fight on our hands."

Four voices spoke up at once.

"She's not disposable."

"Very serious."

"Then I guess we're fightin.'"

"War it is, then."

Reaper laughed through the phone as we did the same around the table.

"I can't imagine Prowler disagreeing with you lot since he's the one that's in there with her now." Reaper took a long breath and breathed it out. "Alright. You all need to be a hundred percent sure because you know what this means for her."

I found myself nodding even though I knew he couldn't see the movement, but Anchor replied for us. "We're sure."

"Then bring her in."

"You got it, prez," Anchor said.

"And get rid of that gun for Emry. I trust him, but we all know how easy it is to distract that kid. I'm gonna send a few more patches your way in case the Capriottis come back, and

I'll post some more around here, too, just to be safe. You guys focus on bringin' her in and gettin' those bikes done."

We hung up soon after that, then sat there for a minute, lost in our own thoughts.

Pulling out my phone, I called Emry. When he picked up, I said, "Come up to the door," and then hung up.

"How do you think Skye's gonna take knowing she has to meet with the prez?" Brawler asked. His gaze was on his hands where they laid in his lap, and though he hadn't said it outright, I knew he wasn't actually asking if Skye would be willing to meet with Reaper; he was asking if we thought she'd agree to be with all of us, tie herself to the club just as much as we were tied to it, which was what her meeting with Reaper was really going to be about.

None of us knew how to answer that, so we were quiet until a knock sounded on Skye's door.

I walked over and opened it, speaking to Emry before I even got the door open all the way. "Give me your gun," I said, reaching out a hand for it when he offered it to me a second later. "Now, go find a burn barrel and set it up out back by the water. You've got an hour, Prospect."

"Sure 'nuff," Emry met my command with his signature naive enthusiasm, which had me rolling my eyes at him and smirking as I shut the door and he took off the stairs outside.

"Now, whose turn is it to make dinner?" I asked, walking back over to the couch. "'Cause, it ain't me."

Chase got up with a sigh and made his way into Skye's kitchen while the rest of us talked and made a plan. He threw in his headphones, probably listening to that Italian opera playlist again while he cooked, blocking us out completely as he worked.

"The real question is," Anchor asked, "Who's gonna knock on Skye's door and tell her she needs to eat when it's ready?"

CHAPTER 14
Skye Sutton

It had never been my intention to shoot Jim when I saw him walking up; I'd just wanted to run again, like I had since I was sixteen, but with everyone else in attendance, that simply wasn't an option. So instead, I was just standing there, panicking on the inside, my gaze unable to leave his as my brain did this thing where it started noticing all of the changes in Jim's appearance that had occurred since the last time I saw him.

His beard was still grimey and dirty looking but had been trimmed. It still had some of that dark brown color it used to be, but it was mostly white and gray now. His eyes were just as dead as they'd always been, but the crow's feet around them had deepened and lengthened. His skin looked... saggy? Was that the word? Like there wasn't as much meat under his bones as there'd been when I lived with him. The suit he was wearing was an entire fucking joke too. He was no man. He was a fucking monster. The same as the day I'd left that house, only now he was older and even more disgusting.

That's what had sent me to the trashcan earlier. It wasn't that I'd killed somebody, which was what I thought all the guys were attributing it to.

No, it was Jim's blood that had dried on my skin and how identical mine could look to his that sent me reeling.

In my head, we were separate, so different from one another that I thought I should've been able to tell a difference between our blood. When the realization hit me that we weren't that different, that he was, in fact, a human just like me and not a monster like I'd built him up to be in my mind, it turned my stomach so hard I might as well have had food poisoning.

I also hadn't intended on breaking down and losing my shit in the shower, especially with Prowler standing nearby, but again, my body hadn't exactly given me a choice; it was just reacting to everything that had happened, and I was at its mercy as it swept through me.

Prowler had handled it well, though. Handled me.

Before I even really knew what was happening, I was wrapped in his arms, and he wasn't judging me for it in the slightest. He just held me, rocked me, and spoke those sweet words in my ear that I already knew I would remember for the rest of my life.

I sobbed for a while, and he allowed me the space I needed to do it, which I also knew I'd never be able to thank him enough for doing.

It was strange how my body reacted to killing Jim. You'd

think, and I did too, that I would've been happy, celebrating even. Ecstatic over the fact that I didn't have to run anymore, or that Jim was never going to hurt anyone else on this gods-forsaken planet, or jumping up and down with the relief of it all, but instead, all I could do was mourn.

Whatever shield of protective armor I'd been wearing since the night I left their house, the one I'd built up and reinforced over time to keep the most vulnerable parts of myself safe in this unsafe world... it just fell away in that shower like it'd never existed in the first place, washing down the drain right along with my tears.

I was exposed. For the first time in twelve years, the child I'd been came rushing to the surface, refusing to stay quiet any longer, and I had no choice but to let her let it all out.

The things that man had said to me, called me, in that parking lot today.

The stuff he'd spewed at me while I'd been growing up.

The way the bruises and scars he'd left looked on my tanned skin.

The way he'd look at me when we were out in public - the way he'd had younger me standing perfectly still, no matter where we were or what we were doing just so he wouldn't hurt Mama and me when we got home because of something I'd done.

The way Mama had always looked out for him instead of me.

Loved him more than she ever loved me.

The look on her face when she turned away from me that night.

My innocence that he'd stolen after she closed the door behind her.

All of it.

I mourned everything.

Every fucking part of it.

Finally.

And Prowler had been right there with me the whole time, never asking questions about why I was crying so hard or trying to get me to talk... he was just there for me when I desperately needed to know that there were good people in this world. His touch grounded me. The hand he was rubbing down the side of my face and the length of my hair as I sobbed into his chest, a perfect example of what touch was supposed to feel like to the human soul.

And when the water started to run cold, and I pulled myself together enough to stand up, that man even started scrubbing my skin for me, washing off the rest of the blood that was still tainting my skin.

Which just made me cry even harder at the disparaging differences between people like Jim and people like Prowler.

I didn't think I deserved what he was doing right then, especially not when he started washing my hair for me as we both froze to death, but I swear to everything good in this world, I loved that man right then and there.

Even my fucking trauma was safe in his arms, and I'd never even dared to dream of such a thing, such a person existing. It was too good to be true for the likes of me. I thought. But here he was, existing and shit. Rinsing the shampoo out of my hair, his blue eyes, understanding and empathetic, proving all of my false beliefs wrong in one long ice cold shower.

"Time to dry off, Little Warrior," he said a short time later, snapping me out of my thoughts, which I was also tremendously grateful for.

"Why do you call me that?" I heard my croaky voice ask as I set myself about the task of grabbing a towel for my hair, one for my body, and one for him off the shelf beside the shower. "I don't feel like a warrior, especially right now."

He took the towel I was handing him and looked down at me with a small smile, his black hair dripping on his eyebrows, as he said, "We might not have fought in any actual wars, but we've both seen battles. Long before we ever should have. I recognized it in you the first time I saw you." He wiped his face, then scrubbed the towel over his head a few times before his gaze settled back on mine. "You're a warrior because you're still here after everything you've been through."

Pushing him in the shoulder lightly, I said, "Dammit, you're gonna make me cry again."

Smirking gloriously, he replied, "And I call you '*Little Warrior*' because look at you." He gestured at me with the towel in his hand. "What are you, like five foot even?"

It felt so good to laugh, even if he was making fun of how short I was.

"I'm a proud four foot eleven, thank you very much. Not all of us can push six feet like you and all those guys out there."

He laughed at that and stepped out of the shower, but

then laughed some more as he jumped right back in because of how much water was dripping off his clothes. "Ah, shit."

Giggling at him, I said, "Hold on. Stay there. I'll go grab your bag from the living room."

"I mean, I would get it, but I'm just gonna ruin your house if I do."

Shaking my head at him, I took a hiccuping breath and started heading to where the rest of the guys were, with one towel wrapped around my body and another twisted around my hair.

When I got in there, all their heads turned to me.

"Which one of these bags is Prowler's?"

It took a second for any of them to respond, which made me smile, but then Anchor got up, grabbed a bag from beside one of the couches, and walked over to hand it to me.

"Thank you," I said sweetly, looking him in the eyes.

"No problem."

Turning on my heel, I went back to the bedroom and heard Chase yell out before I got there, "Dinner will be ready in ten! Get your asses out here by then if you want any!"

———

"What did you put in this stuff?" I asked between fast bites of the alfredo pasta Chase had made. "Crack?" The guys laughed at me. "Fuck, this is delicious."

"Just doing what I can, Sweets," Chase said, winking at me from across my dining room table.

"Well, keep it coming," I laughed. "I'll buy all the groceries you guys could need if it means I don't have to cook while you're here."

Laughing back, Anchor asked, "Why's that?"

"Oh, yeah," I said, "I can't cook for shit."

Laughter erupted around the table, but then I had a sobering thought that raised my eyes to all of those surrounding me.

"Hold on. Now that Jim's dead, you guys are gonna leave, aren't you?"

Anchor's smile only got bigger. "Not a chance," he said. "Jim *was* the problem, but now the whole Capriotti Mafia will have their sights trained on you and this shop. We can't leave yet."

"And we don't want to," Diego said, drawing yet another smile out of me as I looked down at my plate again.

Even more jokes and laughter sounded around the table long after we ate and cleaned up. Surprisingly, everyone was allowed to help this time, and Prowler didn't go into robot mode again like he had this morning. It was a relief, but something I was definitely planning on asking about later when it felt like the right time.

When we were all sitting on the couches, talking and hanging out, a big yawn tore through me right before someone scared the daylights out of me by banging on my side door.

My eyes grew as big as apples, but Diego just laughed as he got up to answer it.

Emry was on the other side of the threshold when Diego opened the door.

"Got it all set up for you, Drifter. Want me to start it?"

"Nah, we've got it, kid," he said before Emry nodded and headed back down the stairs. Then turning all of his attention to me, Diego said, "Get your shoes on, Baby Girl. We've got a job to do."

"What? Why?" I asked. "What kind of job?"

Laughing, he said, "Just go. Come on," with a little nod in my direction.

Huffing because I was tired and really didn't want to go anywhere, I ended up relenting a second later because going anywhere to do anything with Diego sounded like an opportunity I couldn't pass up.

Within a few minutes, I was following him down my outside stairwell and out behind my shop, where a barrel of some kind was sitting in the grass, halfway between the back of my building and the drop-off for the harbor.

When we got up next to it, I saw the pile of blood-stained clothes I'd taken off earlier, along with my favorite boots, lying inside, on top of a few trash bags.

"I figured you'd want to do the honors," Diego said, handing me a stick and a lighter.

"The honors of what?"

"Burning the last bit of evidence tying you to Jim."

I stood there for a second but then took both in hand. Diego grabbed a gas can beside the barrel and started pouring it all over everything inside. Then turning to me, he said, "Dip the stick in here," as he untwisted the cap on the can.

I did what he said, then lit the stick.

"Step back some," he warned with a light hand on my elbow, and without further ado, I tossed the stick into the barrel, watching as it burst to life, flaming high above us.

A few moments later, Diego wrapped a warm arm around my shoulders and pulled me into him. I sent both of my arms around him in response and stood there with my head leaning against his chest.

"I loved those boots," I said, watching as they melted in front of my eyes while the moon beamed down on the two of us, where we stood by the fire, glancing between the flames and the water.

Leaning his head down, he said, "I'll get you some new ones," before he softly kissed the top of my head, and I squeezed him tighter.

"We'll go after work tomorrow. How's that sound?"

"Good."

"After that, you've gotta meet with the prez, though." He sounded almost worried as he spoke.

"For what?"

Sending one of his hands up to push some of the hair in my face behind my ear, he said, "You'll see."

Well, that wasn't ominous, I thought sarcastically.

CHAPTER 15
Skye Sutton

We were standing there for a long time before Emry brought us a couple of the chairs I had in my shop and an even longer time before the flames were done burning through everything. Once it wasn't going to burn our hands off, Diego and I carried the barrel over to the drop-off and poured all of the ashes into the harbor.

I knew it might not have been the best for the environment, but it was the best we could come up with right then.

We stood by the water for a while after that, just hanging out and getting to know each other better. I found out that a lot of Diego's family lived here in Wilmington but that just as many were still back in Mexico. He also told me he had a sister named Carmen, who was two years younger than him, and his mom was throwing a party on Friday for her birthday, which would make her the same age as me. He said everyone was going, and that, of course, meant I was going too.

I didn't argue.

Later, when we were both about to pass out standing there, he walked me upstairs to my bedroom, where Prowler was already posted up, sleeping in the chair Chase had slept in last night.

"I guess he won for tonight," Diego whispered, confusing me.

"Won what?"

Diego turned me by my hips, so I was facing him in the dim hallway of my apartment. "The opportunity to guard you while you sleep."

"That's something to win?" I asked, my eyebrows going straight to my hairline.

He smirked at me, then bent down and brought his lips to mine in this soft, slow kiss that had my skin tingling everywhere. It ended much too soon, but I got over it when he said, "I'll see you in the morning, Baby Girl. Sleep good and dream about me."

Laughing as quietly as I could, I pat him once on the chest. "Same to you."

He kissed me on the forehead, smiling the whole time before I stepped inside my room and closed the door while he made his way back down the hallway.

When the lock made a sound as it closed all the way, Prowler sat up with wide eyes that softened when he saw me. He relaxed back in the chair, but I could not get over how uncomfortable he must've been. Of course, I could've also been afraid to sleep alone tonight, but I didn't want to delve into all that just yet.

Walking over to him, his eyes never leaving mine, I asked, "Will you sleep with me in the bed? I don't want to be alone."

Standing up slowly, he kicked off the boots and cut he'd put back on after changing earlier, followed me over to the bed, and climbed in behind me, so he was closest to the door, just in case.

Wrapping his arm around my belly with his other arm under my head, I snuggled into him, breathing deeper than I thought I had all day, and as sleep took me, I swear I heard him say, "Goodnight, Little Warrior. Tomorrow will be better, I promise."

Sometime in the middle of the night, I woke up to find myself, still half asleep, grinding back into Prowler while his face buried itself in my neck from behind, nibbling and sucking at the tender flesh I had there.

I didn't think I'd ever been as worked up, as turned on as I was at this moment, and part of that, I was sure, was the dream I'd just been having about the guy whose hand was now traveling down my side, sliding into the front of my underwear and sleep shorts.

His tongue was working wonders on that muscle between my neck and my shoulder while his fingers slipped between my folds to dip two tips into me.

"Fuck, Skye," he whispered in my ear. "You're already so wet for me."

"Uh-huh," I got out before he used his body to push my shoulder down to the bed, so I was lying on my back while he propped himself up on one elbow beside me.

Withdrawing his fingers from me a few precious moments later, making me squirm beneath him in protest, he looked me in my eyes and brought his fingers to his mouth to suck and lick my juices off, sending my desire for him even higher.

I couldn't lay there anymore after seeing him do that - something powerful had taken over me, demanding release on my terms, and I wasn't about to ignore it.

Using both of my hands to push him and flip us over, I straddled his frame, loving how his body felt beneath me, how his hands felt as they fell on my thighs, how good he looked in the hint of early morning sunlight that crept into my bedroom and cast shadows across his sculpted features.

Reaching both hands up to either side of my face, he pulled the top half of my body down to his, our lips and tongues touching, twisting, tasting one another as my hair fell around us like a veil, blocking out the whole world.

I could feel his erection pressing into my sensitive flesh, and couldn't help the way my hips rocked over him, teasing both of us with just enough friction to work us up even more.

Pulling away from his kiss so I could sit up, I pulled my top off, baring my chest to him since I wasn't wearing a bra. I was about to start undressing him too, but one of his hands stopped me as he sent his open palm to my lower belly, then slid it up my frame slowly, his eyes following his hand's movement like he couldn't believe he was touching me there.

He stopped when his hand was between my breasts, then moved it back down and to the side, the backs of his fingers grazing the bottom of my left breast, as his other hand came up to mirror its twin on my other side. Then, when they wrapped themselves around my ribcage and squeezed, pushing me down into him even harder, he raised his hips at the same time, increasing the sweet, sweet pressure between our most sensitive parts.

I reached down and started pulling at the bottom of his shirt, but instead of letting me pull it off him, he flipped me onto my back again before he got up and stood at the foot of the bed before me.

"Take those off," he said with a head nod at my shorts and underwear.

A smile spread my lips as I got up onto my knees slowly, sensually, while I held his eyes in my gaze. Hooking my thumbs in the sides of my shorts, I started sliding them down just as slowly, savoring the heat growing behind his eyes as I moved.

When they were at my knees, he said, "Stop," and I lifted back up, arms hanging down beside me. He lifted his hands to undo his belt and jeans, then pulled his long, thick erection out for me to see in all of its glory. "Crawl over here," he said, making my breath hitch in my throat, but I didn't hesitate.

I crawled shamelessly out of my shorts and over to him on all fours, never looking away from his eyes until I was right in front of him. Then, bending down to lay on my elbows so I could reach him better, I lifted one hand to hold his cock where I wanted it, gripping lightly, then sent my tongue out, mouth open wide, to lick around his tip slowly.

His hands fell to my face before he sent his fingers into my hair and combed it to the back of my head so it wouldn't get in the way, all while I wrapped my lips around the head of his dick and gripped him tighter with my hand, sucking hard.

Prowler's whole damn body twitched. The hand he was using to hold my hair twisted with tension, pulling on my scalp as I moved my head back and forth at a pace I knew was driving him crazy. I dropped my hand and went down as far as I could, swallowing around him while he was in my throat a second later.

A sound came out of his mouth from deep inside his chest, and I lapped that shit up like a wanton bitch in heat. Hell, I think my ass could've even shaken in excitement, and it wouldn't have surprised me.

What did surprise me was when he pulled out of my mouth and reached out to flip me over again with two strong hands, then pulled my body even closer to him until my head was hanging off the bed, and one of his hands went straight to pussy.

I took him in my mouth again as my hands grazed up and down the lengths of his arms. He started rocking his hips as he fucked my throat while he worked me into a frenzy at the same time with his deft fingers.

When I was this close to coming in his hand, he stopped,

pulled out of my throat, and I took a gasping breath as I rolled back over on my belly, looking up at him in disappointment because he'd stopped before giving me what I wanted.

The devilish smile on his face told me he knew exactly what he was doing, though, which only caused a smile like that of my own to appear on my lips as I watched him strip before me.

His body was marred with scars of different shapes and sizes, and upon seeing them, my body moved closer to him, coming to a seated position off the edge of the bed while my hand traced over the ones on his chest. Two inch-long lines had been cut into his left shoulder. A long, jagged one ran down half the length of his torso on his right. In addition, I could count six tiny circles at various points on his chest and stomach that formed a random pattern of pain that had been inflicted a long time ago.

I sent my eyes up to his, my hands dormant on his chest.

"Battles, you know?" he shrugged like it was nothing, then bent down to kiss me again.

I knew he was trying to distract me from asking about what he'd been through, and I kind of agreed that now wasn't the best time to bring it up, but still, my heart broke for him.

Prowler pushed me back down to the bed with his kiss while the head of his unsheathed cock moved to wait outside my entrance. He grabbed it with one of his hands and started rubbing it up and down over my folds, sending me into a heady tailspin of want. I mean, I was practically panting when he slowed to a stop and pulled back so he could see me.

"I don't have a condom."

Huffing my frustration, I said, "I'm clean, and on the pill, so I don't mind if you don't."

His smile gave me butterflies, and fire flooded through my veins as he slid all the way inside me with no barrier between us. Gah, he felt so good. I sent my head back to focus my attention on just how good he felt there, but no sooner had my eyes closed than his mouth went to my neck again, and he started moving his hips, overloading my senses in an instant.

His chest fell to rest on mine as he buried his face in my neck and sent both hands down to grab and cup my ass. Squeezing it as he pounded into me, he sent me higher with each and every powerful thrust he made, and all I could do was hold on for dear life to his strong, broad shoulders.

I moaned toward the ceiling, crying out as my release flooded all around him, and he spurted many times over, deep inside me. The whole interaction had been absolute bliss and nothing less.

We laid there for a while like that, getting our breathing back under control while our hands slid slowly over each other's bodies appreciatively.

"You're perfect," he whispered in my ear, then propped himself up on his elbows on either side of me as he stared down into my eyes.

Sending one of my hands up to his lightly scruffy face, I said seriously, "You are too."

CHAPTER 16
Bronx Reynolds - Brawler

We'd all gone to bed, or couch, I guess, really late last night, so when the sun started streaming in through the big glass balcony doors in Skye's living room to fall right on the backs of my eyelids, I got mad at it and rolled over to face the back of the couch I was sleeping on.

But by that point, I was already awake, and there was no chance of me falling back asleep. I'd had a plan since dinner last night that I couldn't wait to set in motion, and as soon as I remembered it, what little sleep I'd gotten didn't matter anymore.

I sat up, checked the notifications on my phone, noticing it was almost 10am, grabbed my go-bag, and went to the guest bathroom to get ready for the day. It seemed like everyone else was still asleep when I got done, so I tried to stay quiet while I moved through her apartment and knocked lightly on her door.

"Just a second," she said, bringing a smile to my face.

That was a guilty as fuck sound if I'd ever heard one. I could also hear them bumping into things, and some whispered yelling after that, which just proved that she and Prowler had been going at it recently. I had to stifle a chuckle as they freaked out, trying to look presentable, I assumed before she opened the door and peered out at me.

"What were you two up to?" I asked like a smartass, smiling like mad.

She grinned hard and blushed, which was an adorable look on her, as she asked, "Wouldn't you like to know?"

"I most certainly would," I said, "but not right now. You need to come with me."

Her face turned puzzled. "What? Why? Where are we going?"

Laughing, I said, "You'll see."

She huffed with a smirk but followed me to her kitchen anyway.

Standing in front of the stove, leaning up against it with my arms crossed over my chest, she looked around for a second, then turned her gaze to me. "What are we doing? They're still sleeping."

Prowler walked by then, heading toward the living room as he said, "Not for long, they're not," before he went over and sat down hard, directly on Anchor's chest.

Anchor tried to shoot up as the breath left his lungs and his eyes went wide, but with Prowler there, he couldn't. Which, in turn, had Anchor shoving at Prowler, and they began to descend even further into their antics, waking everyone else up as they fought it out while I looked back down at Skye.

She was laughing at the scene they were causing, but when I said, "Cooking lesson number one can't start until I know exactly what you can and cannot cook," her eyes were bugging out as she whipped her head back to me.

"What? I don't have time for a cooking class; I'm already late to open the shop. Plus, the last time I tried to make anything, I almost burnt this whole place down and had to throw away the pan."

I wasn't letting her off that easily. "The prospects are already prepping for the day like you had them do yesterday, and we're the only customers you can handle right now, anyway. Now, tell me what you can and cannot cook."

"Listen," she said, both hands moving while she talked, "I can cook some things. I mean, I wouldn't be buying all the ingredients in my fridge if I actually couldn't cook; last night, I'd just meant that I couldn't make things as well as you guys have while you've been here."

I leaned down a bit and said, "Well, we're gonna change that."

Propping her hands on her hips, she asked, "Why do you care?"

"Because when you're with this crew, everybody cooks in a rotation, and I'm not gonna start eating shitty food just because you never cared enough to learn."

"Ouch," she said, sending a hand to her heart in mock outrage.

"Now, go grab the butter and let's get this meal going."

We'd all picked up on how she liked to be told what to do, and I'd been itching to give her my own commands from the moment I realized it. Now, granted, a lot of the commands I'd been fantasizing about were nowhere near the cooking category, but I figured we had more than enough time to get to those if everything played out well.

We made a breakfast hash together with a side of *good, not burnt* scrambled eggs, joking and playing around the kitchen with each other while we cooked and the guys got ready.

Her laughter rang out and echoed through her spacious apartment while we ate, too, bringing smiles to our faces each time we heard it, but before long, we were done eating and letting Prowler do his morning cleaning thing.

"I'm going to get ready for work," she said, her eyes watching Prowler with marked curiosity and concern. I thought about telling her what was up with him but thought better of it a second later because it wasn't my story to tell. He'd let her in on his own time, under his own terms, if he ever did at all. As far as I knew, he'd never told a woman alive about why he was the way he was, and I wasn't about to be the one that let that cat out of the bag before he was ready.

A few hours later, I was hauling a bike that wouldn't even turn on over to one of Skye's workbenches since she'd just finished up with the one that had been there when she stuck her head out of the waiting room door, searched around with her eyes for a second until she found me, then said, "Hey, Bronx. Come in here for a second, please?"

"Am I getting called to the principal's office or something?" I asked as I stood up and started going over to her.

Laughing, she said, "I'd be your principal any day of the week. Just let me grab my ruler."

I chuckled at that and followed her to her office.

She closed the door behind me, gestured for me to take a seat, then went around to the other side of her desk as she said, "I'm about to call Trick, and I thought you might like to speak with him if he has the time."

"Are you serious?" I let myself get way too excited far too quickly, sitting up in the chair fast. "Yes."

She giggled at my enthusiasm while she pulled her cell phone out and called him, then put it on speaker so we both could hear when he picked up.

"Squirt!" he said, and I raised my eyes to Skye's to see she was blushing at the nickname. "It's been longer than a month since you called me, you know that, right? How in the hell am I supposed to sleep at night not knowing if you're okay, huh?"

I leaned back, a grin tearing my face apart because Skye hadn't been lying about knowing him from before she moved here.

"Eh, hmm," Skye said. "Excuse me, but phones work both ways, Trick."

Laughing while some kind of machine whirred in the background, he said, "I keep forgetting that part. Ugh, whatever, Honey. Tell me everything. What's going on over there?"

Skye grimaced at what images that brought to her mind,

I thought, then quickly changed the subject. "Hold on, there's someone here that would like to meet you."

"Ooh," Trick said, "Is it a he? Is he pretty?"

Laughing again, Skye said, "Oh, yeah. He's pretty alright."

"So you *do* think I deserve pretty boy points then?" I asked, resting both arms on the desk between us as I leveled her with a prying glare.

"What? After you made me cook this morning? Oh, hell no. I don't think so." She was smiling hard at me, the little smartass. I loved it.

"Uh, head's up, Pretty Boy," Trick said, getting my attention, "If you ever want Squirt to do something, she can always be bought with chocolate."

"Good to know, Trick, good to know," I said, rubbing my chin with my hand, plotting hard in my head about a Skye/chocolate combo. "Good lookin' out."

"You don't even know Bronx; how are you gonna give him all my secrets in the first five minutes of talking to him?" She sounded outraged, but her face said otherwise, and judging by how Trick responded, he knew that too.

"Oh, you know you love it when guys learn stuff about you and remember it, don't act like you don't."

Laughing some more, she said, "You know me too well, I swear it."

The conversation was pretty easygoing for the next few minutes, but then Skye put me on the spot when she said, "So how do you know of Trick. I mean, I know you grew up in Cali, but I don't know much else."

Sobering some, remembering back to that time in my life, I said, "Well, when I was younger, one of my mom's boyfriends drove a motorcycle to the house all the time, and I was fascinated by it. So one day, to keep me out of their hair, he pulled an Easyrider Magazine out of his saddlebag and handed it to me."

"Oh, no," Trick said. "That wasn't your first introduction to what I can do, was it? I hated that piece."

I chuckled at him. "Yup, that was the one. I can see now why you didn't like it then, but to a kid, somebody who understood what bikes could do, how many ways they could change and look... I mean, I was hooked from that day forward."

"You flatter me, kid, seriously." His voice had turned almost somber, then picked back up again. "I think you've found your own apprentice there, Squirt."

My eyebrows shot up, and I had a whole adrenaline dump, but I wouldn't say anything about how excited I was until Skye gave away how she felt about the topic.

Looking over at me with her own eyebrows raised, a smirk on those sweet lips of hers, she said, "I'm not opposed if that's something you'd want. I mean, you've been working harder than any of these other guys here, but I thought that was just because of your loyalty to the club."

"I would love to be your apprentice." I said, drawing out the word 'love' like I had the first time I met her, but then Trick spoke up before we could say anything else.

"Excuse me, what club is this?" His tone was angry all of

a sudden, and Skye's face squinched up like she hadn't meant to clue him in on the Heathens. At least, not yet.

Trick hadn't been too happy about Skye getting involved with us, but he changed his tune after she told him about everything that had gone down. So there at the end, he was actually thanking the club, through me, for protecting her when she needed it most, even though I told him he didn't need to do that.

Regardless, he was still really concerned about her, and I couldn't blame him. We were definitely pissing off a very powerful organization, even if it did reside on the opposite coast. Trick said he'd do what he could on his end to help keep an eye on the mafia, if such a thing were possible, and keep us updated, but then he had to go because Mike was bringing in a new bike.

When they ended the call, Skye looked over at me.

"Seriously? You want to be my apprentice?"

Smiling, I said, "That's not even a question. Of course, I do. Learning how to do the things you do and spending more time with you too? Sign me the fuck up."

She laughed for a second, then asked, "Won't it mess with your responsibilities for the club, though?"

I shook my head at her. "Not if you're cool with me taking half a day off once a week for club business?" She shook her head, looking confused for a second. "Then, no, working here during your normal business hours shouldn't mess with what I have to do for the club."

"You know this isn't a paid position, right? And you'd

have to apprentice here for at least a year in order for me to hire you outright."

Nodding, I licked my lips. "That makes sense, but I don't need the money anyway. The club pays me and all the guys in our crew. Ever since we took our new positions. But I'm their road captain and collector, so it's not exactly a full-time job that takes up all of my time if you get what I'm saying."

"Alright, you get the go-ahead from whoever you need to, and I'll focus on teaching you while you're here."

"And you get the groceries we need, and I'll focus on teaching you how to cook when we're not here."

Laughing, she stood up and walked around to me. "You've got a deal, Bronx."

"As do you, Skye."

We walked back out into the garage together a few minutes later, joking with each other as we met up with the rest of the guys, but before we could even mention the apprentice thing, one of the prospects, Jacob, came inside looking pretty worried.

"Guys?" he said as he walked up. Anchor nodded his head at him once to get him to start talking. "There was this car sittin' out there for a while with two guys in it, watchin' us. So Emry told me to go ask them what they were doin' here, but they tore off before I got to their window."

"What kind of car was it?" Anchor asked.

"A gray Toyota Camry."

Anchor glanced over to us, then back at Jacob. "What'd they look like?"

Jacob grabbed the prospect cut he was wearing with both hands, hooking his thumbs in the arm holes to rest his arms there. "Like those mafia guys that were here yesterday. Pretty sure I recognized the driver as one of them, at least."

"Alright, thanks, prospect. Go back out and keep watch, and if you see anything else like that, come get one of us immediately."

Jacob went back outside while Anchor turned to us.

"Hold on," Drifter said, rolling his eyes like something stupid had just occurred to him. Then, he pulled out his phone, called someone, and lifted it to his ear while he asked us, "If you were a rich-ass mafia punk stayin' here, where would you book your room?"

Smiles spread around on the faces of each of the guys in our crew as Drifter said, "Hola, Mama. Tengo una pregunta para ti."

Drifter's mom was the manager at the fanciest resort in Wilmington, where we'd all spent a lot of time together while we were growing up. Apparently, a bunch of men had booked three adjoining rooms for a month-long stay under the Caprotti name and were already being a headache for Maria, even though they'd only checked in last night.

As soon as we heard where they were staying, Anchor set about putting a plan in place to see what they were up to and why they hadn't left yet.

I was now the one that was going to take Skye boot shopping and to her meet-up with the prez, while the rest of them went to set up some surveillance at the resort. Maria had been adamant about not bringing our club business there, so the guys weren't going to wear their cuts, but that worked out better for what they were doing since they wouldn't stand out.

When they left at closing time at Skye's, she locked everything up but left the back door unlocked for the prospects and patches that were pulling protective detail while we were gone. I could tell she didn't like doing it but also didn't want them to be without a bathroom or something while she wasn't there, so she did it anyway.

Before too long, Skye was riding behind me with her hands around my waist, sporting a fresh pair of shit-kickers she seemed super excited about, but the closer we drew to the club on my bike, the more anxiety I could feel coming off of her.

In her defense, she really didn't know what she was walking into, and before she agreed to what the prez was going to talk to her about, I wasn't at liberty to discuss anything or give her a head's up of any kind.

Stepping off my bike and handing me her helmet, she said, "You'll be with me, right?"

I stood up and hung our helmets on my handlebars, then turned back around and shrugged out of my cut to hand it to her. "No, but I'll be right outside the doors if you need me."

Sliding into the cut that marked her as my property, she asked, "Why do I get the feeling that I'm not gonna like this one bit?"

CHAPTER 17
Skye Sutton

Bronx led me through the clubhouse, which wasn't anywhere near as packed as it'd been the other night, but still had a number of people milling about, watching us as we walked to a room off the back one we'd been in before.

There were two giant doors to this room, and inside there was a long table with a bunch of throne-like chairs sitting all around it. Reaper was at the head of the table with a bunch of papers in front of him, but he looked up and smiled when Bronx knocked to get his attention.

"Skye," he said, "Come on in and have a seat." Then he nodded at Bronx, which, considering how Bronx gave me a final look, then stepped out without another word, meant 'leave us alone while we talk.'

After the doors closed behind him, I approached Reaper, hesitating before I sat down. This seemed remarkably formal and important, yet also entirely out of left field. No one, Bronx or Diego, had clued me in on what this could be about, and by this point, I was far beyond just curious; I was downright nervous.

"Relax," he said a moment later, his smile softening some under his bright green eyes. "I've asked you here for something very important, but you can breathe at least."

I let go of the breath I had indeed been holding inside my chest, crossed my legs, and sat back in the chair on his right, keeping my hands in my lap until I knew better what to do with them.

"Alright," I said. "What's all this about then? Why all the secrecy?"

Leaning forward, his elbows resting on the table, bunching up his cut near his shoulders, he asked, "Have the boys told you anything about this club's past? About women associated with this club, to be more specific?"

I shook my head at him as my stomach twisted.

He nodded and sat back, relaxing as he took a deep breath of his own.

"Well, I'm sure you know by now that our positions in this club are relatively new, right? That we only stepped into them in the last," he gestured with one of his hands while he tried to pinpoint an accurate timeline, "half-year?"

Nodding back, I said, "Yeah, they've mentioned something like that a few times but haven't shared any real details, and I haven't asked any questions if that's what you're worried about?" my brow furrowed as I talked.

"Eh," he said, "It wouldn't have been a problem if you had or if they did tell you after last night. That's really why you're here now in the first place."

Something told me to stay quiet, so I nodded again and waited for Reaper to explain.

"The women here..." he took another breath, "the ones that hang around, the ones the guys actually date, and even the old ladies that are married to some of the members..." he paused like he was trying his hardest to come up with the best way to spit it out, "before we changed everything, they weren't treated the best. Let's just put it that way."

"What do you mean?"

"Under the old leadership, and even back to our founding, women have always been viewed as property. Property of the club if they hung around a lot, property of an individual biker or crew once they'd been claimed, and that part is still the same. I guess you've got an idea since this is twice now that you've worn one of the boys' cuts."

Smirking with a small, humorless laugh as I repositioned myself to sit up straighter, I said, "Honestly, all I know about what wearing this means came from romance novels and television. The guys also said it would keep anyone around here from messing with me."

"They were right about that," he laughed. "Those boys have never claimed a woman in the entire nine years they've been with this club. That's why everybody was so shocked when Drifter claimed you as theirs; why I had to check with all of them to make sure they were on board with claiming you. Which, I know now, they are, by the way."

A smile I couldn't help formed at his words, but I remained silent while he spoke.

"Anyway, under the old leadership, there were strict rules

about women. For starters, the prez always got special treatment. Meaning it didn't matter if a woman was claimed, married, or nothing. If he wanted to be with a member's woman, he had that right."

I felt myself stiffen in my seat, all traces of a smile gone without a trace.

"That didn't sit well with a lot of the members, but at that time, there was nothing any of us could do about it. Then there were the other rules. Members weren't allowed to tell their partners anything about our club's business because people thought it made them targets or kept them safer somehow, that kind of thing. You could lose your patch altogether if you let them in on anything you did for the club. That separation between members and their partners alone broke up a lot of what would've been happy relationships.

And then there was the rule that, so long as she wasn't claimed, a member could do anything they wanted to any woman they wanted, and it would be fine. I'm sure you can imagine the kinds of issues that caused... a bunch of men with a no holds barred sort of attitude toward the women around here.

Now," he said, shifting in his seat and meeting my eyes. "A lot of us didn't agree with how things were being run here. Not all of it was about how the women were treated, but it definitely had a big role to play, especially after I met and got with Chrissy."

I nodded, following along with what he was saying, remembering his beautiful blonde wife from the last time I was here.

"The leaders were doing a lot of deals without permission or votes from the club by taking products that weren't theirs to line their own pockets too, but that's a story for a different time." Then, taking a breath, he said, "Basically, our old leaders weren't good leaders, and they certainly weren't good men. It took us all a while to see it, but once we did, we couldn't unsee it, you know?"

"I can understand that," I said.

"Well, about a year and a half ago, it all came to a head when the old prez's sights landed on Chrissy."

He had hardly spoken her name, and I knew I didn't like where this was going.

His fists balled in his lap as his gaze drifted to the table while he spoke. "He took her that night, and it damn near took the whole club to keep me from killin' him right then and there. To make matters worse, he wasn't even doing it because he liked her or some such whatever that I could possibly understand. No, he was doing it because I'd pissed him off. It was club politics that got her raped and beaten that night and had it not been for your boys pulling me out, there would've been a hell of a lot more bloodshed than there actually ended up being in the long run."

He blew out a long breath and looked over at me, seeming almost surprised that I was still sitting there and hadn't moved at what he'd just told me.

"We took Chrissy back to Drifter's old apartment, over in Monkey Junction, got her healed up, then set about making the plan for the mutiny. It took about a year to get it done, but that kind of shit didn't happen again, and here we are, running the club the way we think is best. And that starts with throwing many of our old ways out the window and starting fresh with new ideas and ways of thinking."

I nodded, eyebrows raised. "Sounds like you all did the right thing."

He smiled to acknowledge what I'd said, then continued.

"Things are different, but this is still the same club at the end of the day. We tell our women everything. Hell, half the reason the mutiny worked at all was because Chrissy helped us plan it. I swear, the brains on that woman," he laughed a little as he thought about her.

It was cute; I'd give him that.

"But to ensure this club's and everyone's safety within it, we must be given certain assurances. We can't very well go around unloading all of our secrets on girls that these guys don't plan on keeping around; that would be club suicide. However, when our guys are sure of someone, we bring them in here to talk with Anchor or me and go about bringing them 'in' to what we have going on."

"That doesn't sound so bad, but what are these assurances you're talking about?"

Smirking, he said, "Well, we make them just as culpable for what we're doing here as we are. We get their hands dirty in the same deals we do. It ensures their silence when needed, enlists their help with club matters, and makes things run much smoother than they used to, let me tell you."

CILLA RAVEN

He was shrugging this off like it was no big deal, but I wasn't able to laugh it off just yet.

"Culpable, how?"

Laughing, he said, "Usually, I'd say I couldn't tell you anything until you'd agreed to keep your mouth shut, but you kind of already murdered someone, and the club helped you clean it up. You've got blood on your hands, Short Stuff. Mafia blood, at that. We've probably got a war to fight now because of you."

I felt my whole body go rigid. They were going to hold this over my head?

"What exactly are you saying here?"

Leaning toward me, he said, "I'm saying, from the moment Drifter claimed you, you were Heathen property. And if not then, you definitely were when you fired those shots. You belong to Anchor's crew first and this club second. Because of this, they can tell you about everything they're doing without reprimand or expulsion, and you can even offer your advice or skills to help them or the club out as you see fit. You've got a voice here, is what I'm saying."

"What if I don't accept this? What if I don't ask them about anything they do for the club? Could I not be considered property then?"

Panic was welling up inside my chest. Under no circumstances would I ever consider myself someone else's property, except for very specific instances that were all of the sexual variety. The closest I'd ever come was putting on these cuts, but I'd done that more out of self-preservation than anything else. Yes, it was nice to feel like I belonged to each

of the guys, especially when they were saying it while we were in the heat of the moment, but to actually be 'owned' by them? By this club? The prospect scared the hell out of me.

Chuckling darkly, Reaper said, "You gave up your right to accept or not the moment you pulled that trigger, and Anchor shot the Capriotti Mafia don's son in the leg to end your debt. Now, it's not up for debate. We really have no interest in outting you to the cops or turning you over to the Capriottis, or whatever that look on your face says you're worried about," he paused as he looked me in the eyes, "but you need to know that if I have to, I will. If it comes down to you or this club, this club will always win."

"So," I started, closed my eyes, and breathed out hard through my nose. "It doesn't matter what I want. I belong to them, to you, to this club... all of it."

"Yes."

I sat forward and ran my hands through my hair. "This sounds like my worst nightmare."

Laughing, he said, "I promise, it's not that bad, and really, we're getting rid of more and more rules all the time. Who knows? Maybe you'll be the one to change the whole 'property' topic, but for right now, yes, what you're saying is correct."

I ran through a bunch of different scenarios in my head, but the one that screamed the loudest was what I asked next.

"I haven't found a reason not to yet, but what if things don't work out with me and the guys? What then?"

His face turned serious as he regarded me.

"Let's just hope we don't have to cross that bridge."

Sitting back, my attitude bursting out at the seams, I said, "No, how 'bout not? What will happen?" I was practically yelling at this point, but he didn't answer me before his phone started ringing in his pocket.

"Hello?" he said, holding a finger up in my direction that I really wanted to break right then. His face turned angry, but his voice sounded almost pleasant as he spoke to whoever was calling him. "Ah, Mr. Capriotti. I thought I might be hearing from you soon."

Shocking the hell out of me, he pulled the phone away from his ear and put the thing on speaker.

"...my brother, Carl."

"Well, John," Reaper said with a smug set to his chin. "I don't know exactly what you expected. You sent a bunch of guys into my territory with no courtesy call, threatened my boy's woman, demanded money that never even belonged to that Jim guy, and you're surprised when we shot your brother? Come on, you know how these things go. You would've done the same, I'm sure."

"But it wasn't me," the guy I assumed was Carl's brother, John Capriotti, said. "So, here's what's going to happen. The money that Jim owed us has now become your club's debt. To be exact, your club is now on the hook for seven and a half million." He paused briefly, then said, "Plus a collector's fee for all the trouble you've caused."

Reaper's face was as angry as I thought it could get, and

all I could do was sit there and listen as his words sealed my fate for me.

"The Raging Heathens don't owe you or your family anything. Skye Sutton doesn't owe you anything, either. She is under our protection, just as much as any Heathen."

Sounding almost bored, like how his brother had sounded yesterday, John said, "Well, I guess you know what this means," and then he sighed.

"If it's an east coast, west coast, MC, mafia war you want, you've got it, but you're not getting a dime out of any of us, that's for damn sure." Reaper was standing up now, hands on the end of the table, staring down at his phone. He looked positively terrifying right then.

"It's been a pleasure, Ronald. We'll be in touch."

John hung up then, and call me crazy if you want, but I had to fight off a giggle at the fact that Reaper's name was Ronald.

He'd heard me, though, and sent his angry gaze to mine.

A sound came out of my nose that I just could not help as I sent a hand to my mouth.

"You're just like your guys, you know that, right?"

The laugh tore out of me a second later, and surprising me even further, Reaper started smiling too. "Sure thing, Ronald."

Pointing a half-assed finger in my direction, he said, "That's the only time I'm letting you get away with calling me that. Do it again, and I'll sic your guys on you or something." He stood up straight and readjusted his cut over his torso. "Nobody's called me that since I was a kid, dammit."

Giggling because I didn't know what else to do, I stood up and sent my hand out to his.

"I may not like being anyone or anything's property, but like you said, I have a voice here, and really, that's my biggest hangup. Otherwise," I turned serious, "I know what you did for this club and for me just now, and I don't take it lightly. Whatever I can do to help, I'm here for it, Ronald."

He looked angry for a split second, then smirked, sending his hand into mine in a firm shake. "Just fucking like them, I swear," he said with an eye roll that had me laughing all over again as we both started heading back out into the clubhouse.

———

The rest of the week passed by in a blur of work and worry. More cars had been spotted staking out my shop and the clubhouse, but because of Diego's hook-up with the resort that the mafia guys were staying at, they'd been able to set up their own kind of recon. I hadn't asked about anything they'd seen or heard, but I knew I could've asked if I wanted to.

Instead, I threw myself into my work and painting and hanging out with the guys. Not once did they treat me like property, which I was grateful for, but then again, nothing had really happened for that trump card to come into play.

However, when Friday afternoon rolled around, Bronx came up to me and asked, "You know that half day I need every week for club business?"

"You need to go?" I guessed.

Smiling, he said, "*We* need to go."

"What? Me too?"

"Yup. How else are you gonna know what we do? It's not like you ask us a whole lot of questions where the club is concerned."

Huffing with a smirk, I said, "That's intentional. What I don't know can't hurt me, right?" being sarcastic as fuck.

His face turned serious. "It most certainly can, and we're not willing to let you live in ignorant bliss anymore. You need to know what you've gotten yourself into."

I knew he made a good point and that by trying to avoid anything that had to do with the club other than the guys and the bikes I was working on, I was just dragging out what was already inevitable.

"Fine, I'll go with you, but who's gonna look after the shop?"

He looked around the garage, where everyone was pulling their own weight.

"Woman, you've got this place running like a well-oiled machine. Anchor and the rest of 'em can handle us being gone for a few hours. Have some faith in what you've already taught us."

That smile... ugh, I couldn't say no to it.

The next thing I knew, I was riding bitch behind Bronx as he tore through the streets of Wilmington. As soon as we left, he took my left hand in his and held them both over his heart for some reason, but I didn't mind. It was like he was forcing me to cuddle into his back; truth be told, that's where I wanted to be anyway.

He pulled up to some random house in a small subdivision a short time later, took both of our helmets, and said, "You're free to stay here, or you can come with me. It's your choice," as he pulled this long, thick stick thing out of one of his saddlebags. "I've gotta warn you, though, you might want to stay at a good distance this time, just in case."

"Why? What are you doing?"

He just smirked before he started walking down the street. I climbed off his bike and trailed behind him until he found the house he wanted. Once we were there, he passed right by the front door, circled the house, and let himself in through the back door.

Bronx never stopped moving as I noticed we were in somebody's kitchen, and he hit the stick thing against his palm a few good times, yelling, "Oh, Paco!"

All I could see was Bronx's back, and all I could hear was some guy in the living room saying, "Oh, shit," before he took off through the front door, and Bronx ran after him. I didn't want to be left standing in some rando's house, so I ran after them.

Bronx chased him around to the side of his house and, in one swift motion, used that stick thing to swipe at the back of the guy's knees, sending him tumbling down to the concrete pad of his driveway.

Standing over him and leaning down, Bronx held the stick in front of the guy's face and said, "Paco," warningly.

Paco stopped struggling and put his hands up by his face.

"What's the rule, Paco?"

Was Bronx smiling? And why is it giving me butterflies to watch him do this?

"Come on, man. It's hard out here, you know that."

Bronx pushed the stick down hard into Paco's chest and leaned his weight down.

"Fuck, fuck, alright, shit!"

"What's the rule, Paco?"

"Don't sell to kids!" Paco yelled back at Bronx right when I noticed the red bandana hanging out of Paco's pocket.

Removing the stick from Paco's chest, Bronx said, "That's right. Now, if you knew that, why are you still hanging around the school, sellin' to teenagers when you know better, Paco? You had to know this was gonna happen."

"Please, Brawler, just let me go. I won't do it again, I promise!" the guy pleaded, and I knew I wasn't involved, but in my head, he sounded serious. Though, maybe, he was just trying to save his own ass.

Bronx's voice turned deadly. "You better not. This is your last warning. Do you understand me, Paco? Say you understand."

Paco nodded and vehemently said, "I understand, boss, I promise."

Bronx stood up like he was going to let Paco up but then whacked the fuck out of Paco's side once. Paco curled in on himself, and I was sure Bronx had cracked a rib or two with that strike, at least. Then he backed up a few steps and asked, "Now, where's the drop?"

From what I could tell, Paco was doing everything he could not to cry as he fought his way to his feet and pointed at the house we'd just run through.

"It's on the table, man, shit."

Crossing his arms over his chest, Bronx asked, "You think I'm going back in there to get it?" He took a menacing step toward Paco. "Move your ass." The words were barely out of his mouth before Paco started running as best he could back into his house, sending a joke of a smile my way as he passed me. Bronx walked up to join me, took my hand in his, and led me back to Paco's front yard as Paco ran out with a white envelope in his hand. He gave it to Bronx, who tucked it safely into his cut.

"I'm sorry, man. It won't happen again."

Bronx didn't even acknowledge what Paco had said; instead, he turned us around and started walking us back to his bike like this was some leisurely afternoon stroll rather than... whatever that had just been.

"The Heathens have a few rules we aren't getting rid of, and that's one of 'em," Bronx explained as he climbed on his bike and held my helmet out to me.

I might not have known exactly what Paco had been trying to sell to kids or who those kids were, but it seemed like a pretty solid rule to me, so I just nodded while I climbed behind him, and he pulled my left hand to his chest again when he took off.

As it turned out, that was the only violent encounter we had for the rest of the day.

The rest of the places he took me to collect what, I assumed, was cash seemed almost monotonous by the time we were done. Everywhere he went, all he had to do was drive up, and someone was coming out with their own envelopes and handing them to him. A few smiled at me, but no one really spoke during the interactions, which did unnerve me a little.

We stopped by a couple of houses, two strip clubs, a few restaurants and bars, a laundry mat, and what could've only been described as a chop shop hidden inside the back of a landfill. Bronx would take what they gave him, slide it into his saddlebag, and take off again, taking no longer than a few minutes at each location; however, before I knew it, we were back at the shop, and Diego was walking up to me while I crawled out from behind Bronx.

"Time to get ready," he said while I tried to tame my hair from being inside a helmet for a while.

"Ready for what?"

"My sister's birthday party."

———

"What's this?" I asked Diego a bit later as he followed me into my room. A short, white spaghetti strap dress was lying on my bed, along with a pair of strappy silver heels.

He walked up behind me, slid his hands over my hips, then latched them together in front of me while dropping his head to rest on my right shoulder. "I didn't know if you had anything other than shorts and tank tops, so I got you this for tonight."

Indignant, I said, "I have dressy clothes too."

"You just never wear them."

Sighing because I really did want to try it all on, I said, "This is very thoughtful; thank you."

Leaning his face down, he kissed my neck before I turned around, smiling, and shoved him out of my room so I could get ready in my ensuite while they all had to fight over the guest bath to do the same.

Really, I had no idea what to expect for this party, but judging by the fancy/casual style of the dress he'd bought me, I figured I needed to at least give my makeup and hair a good seeing to. So, after showering, I threw on just enough makeup to make it look like I wasn't wearing any, plus a little mascara for some added pop then blow-dried and curled my hair loosely, so it fell in long, flowing waves around my face and down my back.

When I put on the dress with a white strapless bra, I knew Diego either had a good eye for women's clothes, or he'd gone through my closet to be sure he got the right size because it fit perfectly. Tight around my breasts and midsection, its loose, flowing bell shape stopped just above my knees and swayed gracefully when I moved. The heels had velvet on the bottoms of them, which I didn't understand, and the heel seemed like it sat further in toward the center of the foot than most heels I'd ever worn. They fit just as perfectly as the dress, though, so I wasn't complaining as I looked myself up and down in the mirror one good time.

When I stepped out of my room, all the guys' eyes landed on me with different expressions, and I almost tripped. We'll say it was because I wasn't used to how slippery the velvet was on my smooth tile floor, and it certainly wasn't caused by how having all of their attention on me at once made me feel.

They were still dressed in their cuts, but they'd showered, put on some nice jeans, and smelled absolutely delicious as we made our way down the stairs and out to the bikes.

"She's riding with me this time," Chase said, making me smile, and a round of 'ugh' sounds could be heard from the other men. Still, when he handed me a helmet and climbed on his bike, I couldn't help but feel all kinds of sexy and wanted as they watched me climb on in my short dress. It was like I could literally feel their eyes on me while I moved, and it prickled my skin in all the best ways.

Chase's hand rested on my left thigh the whole ride over to Diego's mom's house, rubbing lightly every now and then, squeezing here and there, too.

I was only a tiny bit worried about my hair but got over it quickly since I thought the helmet might actually help accentuate the curls... At least, that was my hope, anyway.

As it turned out, though, once we walked inside, I forgot all about my hair entirely.

People were everywhere, drinks were held in almost every hand, and children ran around having a blast with some

Nerf guns. Both the front and back doors were wide open for people to come and go as they pleased, and we could hear music playing in the backyard, even though we hadn't gotten there yet.

Diego sent a smile over his shoulder at me as he grabbed my hand and started pulling me through the open-concept space to the kitchen area, where he stopped before a beautiful older woman that was just a hair shorter than me.

"Mama," Diego said as he bent down to kiss her cheek, and the rest of the guys settled in around us.

She hugged him back, then her eyes, which were a perfect match to her son's, landed on me. "You brought a girl, Mijo?" she asked Diego, grabbing both of my hands in hers while she looked over to the other side of the kitchen and said, "Carmen! Diego brought a girl!"

"What?" the female version of Diego said like she couldn't believe what she'd just heard.

"What's your name?"

"Skye," I smiled down at her as she raised a hand to my face for a brief second, then turned her attention to her son.

"Why didn't you tell me you were bringing her?"

"Call it a surprise," Diego said with a shrug. "Skye, this is my mom, Maria. Come now, Mama, let her go. I haven't even shown her around yet."

Turning to look back at me, she said, "You're not going anywhere until you eat something. Look at you." She gestured to me like I should know what she was talking about, but I was just so overwhelmed and smiling so hard I thought my cheeks were going to hurt that I couldn't have denied her if I tried.

She led me over to the counter, where she immediately started making me a plate and refused to let me help. "Do you like these?" she asked, but she didn't give me a chance to respond before she said, "Ah, I'll just give you some of everything. How about that?"

I just nodded as Brawler walked between us and kissed Maria on the cheek. "Hey, Mama. I'm gonna head out and get a beer. You want anything?"

She blushed hard at him but waved the serving spoon in her hand at him. "No, no, you go."

He squeezed her in a sideways hug, winked at me, then headed out the back door to our left. Then, seeming to follow his cue, Anchor, Prowler, and Chase did the same, kissing her cheek as they passed her and headed outside.

Diego stayed by me when she yelled out after them, "Make sure you come back and get some food, boys!"

I couldn't help it; a happy giggle raced through me.

I'd been in this house for all of five minutes, and already it was like I was witnessing what a real family was supposed to feel like, how mothers were supposed to act, and the whole situation just made me giddy.

She handed me a fork and my plate and said, "You come sit next to me." She put a hand on my lower back to guide me out the back door. "Mijo," her head had whipped around to a smiling Diego, who was following right behind us. "Go get your ladies something to drink. We're thirsty already; look at us."

Laughing at that right along with her, we finally got over to where some tables and chairs had been set up on the left-hand side of the yard, while on the right, a dance floor had been erected with a DJ booth and everything. Even string lights twinkled between all the trees surrounding the fenced-in yard. It was gorgeous, from top to bottom, and everything was perfect - the lighting, the people, the conversations, the food, the music, everything.

The guys came over to sit with us once they'd made their plates, and our conversation swayed easily from one topic to another between all of us.

Laughing a short time later, I asked, "How did you all get your call signs anyway?" Then, pointing a fork toward Anchor and Prowler, I asked, "And what are your real names? I've never heard them."

Maria busted out laughing with a glorious smile as she said, "You know these boys have been spending every summer at my job with me since they were kids. Well, except for this one." She sent a hand out to pat Bronx's back. "He came a bit later, but we still love him."

"Love you too, Mama," Bronx said with a smile before he took another bite of his food.

"They used to love Chase's dad's motorcycle and the club so much; it was all they talked about."

"Yeah, it used to drive me nuts," Carmen said from my left, with this forced blase attitude that quickly gave way to a full-on smile a second later.

"They had their names picked out... Oh, when was that, Carmen? Tenth grade?" Maria said.

"Sounds right to me." Carmen nodded.

"We all wanted our road names to be like our real names so they wouldn't get confusing, so we looked up as many words as we could that started with the same letter as our real names and made a habit of calling each other by them all the time," Anchor said.

"But you see," Carmen interjected, "In their little club, you're not supposed to get a road name until you get patched, but these guys," she playfully pushed at Diego's shoulder, "have never played by the rules a day in their lives, so they've been called by their chosen names from day one."

"This one," Maria said, gesturing her hand across the table from us to Prowler. "His name is beautiful. Princeton. Like the school." She brought her hand up to her heart while *Princeton* blushed and smiled at her. "At the beginning, it was just these two. My Diego and Princeton, running all over the resort all summer long. Oh my gosh, I could not keep up with them." She paused for a moment and turned her body to face me more fully.

"He had to go to school up in Virginia every year, but over the summers, those two were inseparable."

Looking over at Prowler, I said, "I thought you all went to school with each other?"

Shaking his head a little, a sad look developed on his face out of nowhere, it looked like he was about to say something, but Maria spoke up first.

"Oh, the rest of them did, sure." She nodded. "But Princeton's father lived in Virginia and put him in boarding school there every year. These boys, though, with how much they talked on the phone or sent things back and forth to that school, it was like they were never apart. He moved down here when he was sixteen, though, and then they did go to school together."

Nodding, I just took in all this information I hadn't known I'd been dying to know until I heard it.

"Now, that one," Maria pointed to Anchor. "He's August. Such a good boy."

I smiled at how sweet this woman was, at how much I could tell she cared about all of them.

"He had to do a lot for his family. It'd been very tragic."

"Mama," Diego said, clearing his throat, trying to get her to stop, I imagined, but Anchor chimed in, setting everyone at ease.

"It's okay, Drifter. I don't mind."

He sat back in his chair and sent a hand out to Maria so she'd continue.

The woman was so excited to tell me about him that she almost bounced.

"Oh, see?" she asked, "Such a good boy. And he had to be. He's got two younger siblings, and they were just as cute as him, I tell you. But back when his father passed, his Mama was working three jobs, three," she held that many fingers up to accentuate her point, "You know she could not be there all the time. You understand."

I nodded.

"So he fed those babies, he cleaned that house, he made sure they got to school with clean clothes on. You never saw those kids looking like he let himself look." She laughed a little, and August smiled as he resituated himself in his seat. "When it was summertime, they would all go over to his house to help. Now, those kids, now they're in Ivy League colleges, you hear? August and his mama did such a good job with them." Her voice had turned so proud she had to send the back of her hand up to wipe at her eyes that had gotten teary while she talked.

"Yeah," Carmen said, pulling my eyes to hers, "It's all fun and games until you've got all five of them bossing you around like you're their kid." She stuck her tongue out at all of them around the table, laughter erupting from everyone at the same time.

When I was done eating my fill of the incredible food Maria had made a little while later, Diego took my plate to the trash, then came back over to me and reached a hand out in my direction.

"Oh," Maria said, drawing out the sound into a small squeal that I couldn't help but blush at as I took his hand and let him lead me to the dancefloor, where people were salsa dancing so well, I felt like an imposter, just stepping up there with him.

I didn't consider myself a bad dancer by any means, and Trick had shown me a few basic steps a few years back, but still, nerves were pounding through me. However, I didn't have a chance to get all self-conscious before Diego pulled me into him and led me around so well he actually made it look like I knew what I was doing.

Every time he spun me, I giggled, loving how the cool

night air felt in my hair as it whipped around after me and how it flowed through the fabric of my dress.

We danced for a while, and honestly, I didn't think I'd ever had that much fun with anyone in my entire life. I couldn't get over it; how happy I was. It was like a dream. Like a perfect dream that I never wanted to end, and when Diego said we were leaving this party to head over to one that was in full swing at the clubhouse, it seemed like they didn't want this night to end either.

CHAPTER 18
Skye Sutton

We made it to the clubhouse a short ride later, and Diego was doing that thing where his eyes were lingering on mine.

"What?" I asked, handing him my helmet so he could hang it on his bike.

"I'm just really glad my mom likes you. This would've been real weird if she didn't approve." He laughed and pulled me into his chest for a hug as August's phone rang.

"Yeah, Prez?"

Pulling away from Diego, we all watched as August's face went from smiling at Diego and me to downright livid in the span of a heartbeat.

"We're already here." He sighed. "We're on our way."

If I hadn't known before, I sure as shit knew something was up as soon as we walked in.

"Hang arounds! Get out!" Reaper called from somewhere in the back, and instantly, the place was filled with hushed tones as some people stayed and others went out onto the porch outside.

Each of my guys was tight-lipped and wasn't joking like they usually would. None of them had even given me their cut to wear as we walked inside. However, since Diego was practically dragging me back to the room where I'd met with Ronald, no one even got a chance to say or do anything untoward.

Walking inside, they had me sit beside Princeton while the rest took their seats. As I looked to the end of the table at Ronald, I got a feeling that whatever this was, it wasn't good, but I didn't say anything so he would.

"Here's what I know from our guys watching the Capriottis at the resort," he started. "They're planning on following you back to Skye's shop as soon as you leave here tonight. I guess they found out about the party we were throwing somehow. That's why I hoped to catch you before you got here, so you could avoid them. They're going to ambush you en route and take her back to California."

"What?" I asked, dread and terror surging through me in equal measure.

"Not if we figure out a way to stop 'em first," August said, looking angrier than I'd ever seen him.

Everyone was silent for a second, but then Diego spoke up. "How many of them are there?"

"Two cars with eight men. Carl's going to be with them. They're already staged somewhere close by, but our guys didn't hear where exactly."

"Alright," Diego said. "What if we trap 'em?"

"How?" Anchor asked.

"We send a decoy crew out, pretendin' to be us. Let the mafia follow them where we tell the decoy group to go, then we could fall in quietly behind them in the van. We could have the decoy crew turn down that street off of River Road past the curve, and let them think we're trapped, then we could follow in behind them in the van, trapping them instead."

Nodding, Ronald said, "That could work." He thought for a second. "If we do this, it'll be blackout, no cuts. I don't want anyone seeing this and tying it to us if we can help it."

Everyone was quiet for a minute, but Ronald broke the silence when he asked, "All in favor?" and each of the guys' hands went up. "Alright, let's get this thing movin' then."

I didn't know why I said it, but I did. "I want to be there."

Smiling, Anchor said, "Of course, you're coming. I want you to see the look on Carl's face when we handle this thing with him once and for all."

Apparently, my white dress was just what we needed to make Diego's decoy idea work. A member's girlfriend was wearing a similar one, partying at the clubhouse already. When given a choice to be a part of whatever was going down, she jumped at the chance immediately and onto the back of Diego's bike behind some guy I hadn't met yet.

Chrissy came up to me then while we were standing just inside the doorway, waiting for the decoy crew to leave. I guessed she saw all the worry on my face.

"It'll be okay," she said, sending a hand to my back.

"This life is hard, but these guys are smart. They know what they're doing."

I nodded because I couldn't think of anything else to do as I watched the decoy crew pull off.

I'd been hoping no one would start following them, but almost as soon as they pulled through the gate and turned right, two cars passed by with what looked like blacked-out windows, making my stomach sink.

"Let's go," Diego said as we all ran out to a van they had parked outside and climbed in. August was driving, Diego was in the passenger seat, Chase was on my right, Bronx on my left, and Princeton was across from me in the seats that ran down the lengths of the van.

Sending a pistol my way, Princeton said, "Put this somewhere, and when we get there, stay inside and keep your head down."

"Where am I supposed to put it?" I asked as I took it, staring at it with wide eyes.

"How tight is the pair of underwear you're wearing?" Chase asked with a chuckle.

Sending a smartass glare at him, I asked, "What underwear?" which had an almost ravenous look tearing across his features.

"Seriously?" he said as an evil smile spread across his lips. "Let me see." He reached his hand out playfully, and I smacked it away in kind.

"Just hold it then," Princeton said, smiling as he checked the other gun he had on him.

I wanted to keep talking or something. Keep their spirits

high. But it seemed like the closer we got to wherever we were going, the quieter and stiller they became. By the time we were turning and slowing to a screeching halt, each of the faces I could see was full of nothing but complete impassivity, with no emotion anywhere in sight.

They jumped out of the van in a hurry, and as soon as the first shots rang out, I did as they said and stayed low, crouching behind the passenger seat Diego had just vacated. A few shots hit the van somewhere, but soon they were all directed elsewhere, and I risked a peek through the windshield.

The two cars I'd seen earlier were parked in a V formation, one veering off to the left and one to the right in what I assumed was some sort of tactic to keep the decoy crew from escaping. Ahead of them were the guys' five bikes, but half were blocked from my line of sight because of the mafia's cars.

All the guns had stopped firing within seconds of starting, which had really felt like hours.

Bodies were lying around the cars on the ground, but as I quickly accounted for each of my guys and those of the decoy crew, a breath of relief so strong it blew the hair out of my face flowed out of me.

Anchor called out half a second later. "Skye!"

I didn't miss a beat; I climbed out and ran over to them with both hands wrapped around the pistol Princeton had given me without a backward glance. When I made it over to where they were standing at the front of the car on the left, I saw that Carl was on his knees, and they were holding him at gunpoint.

He was wearing these dumbass-looking shorts, exposing the huge bandage wrapped around one of his thighs. The look on his face when he saw me was pure rage if I'd ever seen it, but I didn't let that bother me as I stepped up to Diego's side, who was the closest to me at the time.

"All the rest of your guys are dead. The only reason we're leaving you alive is so we can try and squash this shit between our club and your family," August was saying.

However, Carl never took his eyes off me or acknowledged that August was speaking to him in the first place. Then, I guess Diego sensed something was off with how Carl started smiling at me, too, because he took a step to his left to stand between Carl and me.

The next thing I knew, a gunshot rang out, and hot blood spurted out of Diego's back and onto me, splattering all over the white dress I was wearing. Again, my fight or flight system kicked in, and everything slowed.

I looked down at Diego's back right as he started to fall to his knees in front of me while other shots rang out, and I automatically knew Carl was dead without even having to look his way.

My body moved on its own, wrapping my arms around Diego before he could hit the ground, but then I wasn't able to hold his weight and mine at the same time, so I ended up falling to the ground with him anyway. I rolled him over onto his back quickly. I immediately started putting pressure on the spot where he'd been shot, as absolute chaos then erupted all around, tears beginning to stream out of my eyes as I stared into Diego's.

Laughing a little while obviously in a lot of pain, he reached up a hand to my face to wipe one of my tears away with his thumb, then his eyes closed, and a sob tore through my chest - the likes of which I'd never experienced in my life.

Epilogue

JOHN CAPRIOTTI

(One Month Later)

"We brought you a gift," I said to Grizz, the Risen Demons' general, while my boys unloaded a freshly stolen shipment from the Raging Heathens' shipyard.

Crossing his arms over his chest, gun in hand, he asked, "I know you ain't givin' somethin' for nothin.' What do you want for this?"

Smiling and clasping my hands in front of me, I said, "Your gang has the best distribution on the east coast - a market we'd like to dip our hands in. The only problem for us seems to be the same one you have."

"And what's that?"

"Your roads are swarming with loud, obnoxious, leather-clad bikers, and from what I hear, they're not paying you as much as you could be earning if you were to work for us instead."

Smiling like I'd struck the nerve I wanted to, Grizz asked, "How much more?"

"Thirty percent."

"Shit," Grizz said, "That's double what we're gettin' from the Heathens now."

"Right."

"So what's your plan then? 'Cause, we ain't takin' out two clubs no matter how much you pay us. There's just no way."

Nodding, I said, "It wouldn't be so hard to let them kill each other off, though, would it?"

"What do you mean?"

Stepping closer and wrapping an arm around Grizz's shoulder, I looked over to where brick after brick of cocaine was being unloaded from our van and into his warehouse. "I mean, if we could get the Heathens and the Savages to get wrapped up in their own war, they'll never see this coming."

"How are you plannin' on doin' that? Aren't the clubs all buddy-buddy now? Runnin' guns and shit?"

Withdrawing my arm, I looked at Grizz and clasped my hands together again.

"That's where you come in. I need you and your Demons to drive a wedge so thick into their newfound alliance that they have no choice but to start fighting each other. Then, once both of their packs are so small they can hardly bark, we'll step in and take over their combined territories, making you our sole distributor for the entire area east of the Mississippi.

Grizz laughed like mad, as I would imagine someone would laugh if they won the lottery. Then turning to me when he got his emotions back under control, he said, "What's funny is, I know exactly where to start."

"Oh?" I asked, genuinely curious.

"Yeah," Grizz said. "The Savages have this prospect, right? We see him all the time, runnin' up to school in Jacksonville five days a week. We can start this thing there if we make it look like a Heathen hit."

"We can start this there," I said, shaking Grizz's hand as *our* new alliance was finally formed.

Also by Cilla Raven

Beholden To Balance

Initiate

Reign

Hunter

Defender

The Fae Bounties

Shameless Fae

Reckless Fae

Lost Savages MC

Wake

Take

Raging Heathens MC

Drifter

Prowler

Hallows

A Date With Death: Part One

Shared Worlds

Sneaky As A Fox

Lexi

Drifter

I sincerely hope you loved Drifter. If you enjoyed the book, I would really appreciate **an honest review** because they help so much! Thank you!

To get an immediate notification when I have a new release, please **sign up for my mailing list!**

To see the complete reading order for this series and to dive into all of my book worlds, **visit my website!**

About the Author

Cilla Raven is an indie author that lives in Montana with her husband, children, and a few fur babies.

You can find all of Cilla's books, merchandise, and more on her **website**!

Love Cilla's books? **Join her mailing list** to be notified of new releases, giveaways, and more!

She'd love to have you join her **Facebook group**: *The Raven's Nest - A Cilla Raven Reading Group.* You'll get exclusive updates and teasers, live streams with Cilla over coffee, and all the funny memes you can stand. **Join now**.

Acknowledgments

First and foremost, I would like to thank you, the reader, for reading my book! It really does mean the world to me!

If you've got a second, would you mind leaving a review telling me what you thought of this book? Reviews are everything, and when you leave them, you make it possible for indie authors like me to keep writing the books we all know and love.

I'd like to thank Nichole, my fantastic cover artist and friend, for making such a beautiful cover, as well as for befriending me in this crazy author world - you're the best!

To my Canadian twin and freakin' amazing PA, Sarah, whose stuck with me through all of my life's crazy ups and downs over the last few years. I couldn't do this without you, seriously. I love you, lady!

To my fantastic alpha and beta teams. You guys have helped me so much, I can never thank you enough!

To my amazing family and friends for supporting me through each and every step this path has taken me.

Again, thank you so much for reading this book, and please feel free to share it with your friends, leave reviews and rate it wherever you can, and let me know what you think!